Who's Counting?

Who's Counting?

A Real-Life Account of People
Changing Themselves and
Their Company to Achieve
Competitive Advantage

Jerrold M. Solomon

WCM Associates
Fort Wayne, Indiana

Who's Counting?

By
Jerrold M. Solomon

WCM Associates
P.O. Box 8035
Fort Wayne, IN 46898-8035
260-637-8064
www.wcmfg.com

ISBN 13: 978-0-9662906-2-2
ISBN 10: 0-9662906-2-3

Front and rear cover design by:
Pro-Art Graphic Design
928-708-9445

Book and text design by WCM Associates
Printed and bound by:
Thomson-Shore, Inc.
Dexter, MI
(734) 426-3939

Layout was completed using Adobe(R) Pagemaker 7.0.
Text typeface is Times New Roman, 11 point.

Library of Congress Catalog Card Number: 2003100324

*To my wonderful wife, Sheila, who
has been my inspiration for more
than twenty-four years
and to my children,
Scott, Aimee, and Whitney,
who have made each and every day
of my life an adventure.*

Acknowledgments

This book would not have been possible without the help and continued encouragement of a number of colleagues. First, I'd like to thank MaryPat Cooper, the Lean Champion at Brooks Electronics, a division of Wiremold. MaryPat has been tirelessly leading the effort at this world-class facility for many years and has always welcomed my visits to learn as much as I could from her. Her insights, encouragement, and continual guidance through numerous rewrites were invaluable.

I'd like to thank the folks at the Maryland World Class Manufacturing Consortium, (MWCMC), a unique organization funded by the Maryland Department of Business and Economic Development. The MWCMC is a world-class organization in its own right for its groundbreaking efforts assisting Maryland manufacturing companies with their Lean journey. I'd like to express my gratitude to Roger Satin, the Director, and John Zyrkowski, the consortia's consultant, for providing me with ongoing guidance and continual access to world-class companies and seasoned Lean practitioners.

My efforts to convert from traditional accounting practices to Lean accounting would not have been possible without the help and support of Christy Martin, Director of Information Technology, John Walter, Director of Manufacturing, Howard Lin, Financial Analyst, and Tom Hampton, Controller at PACE, Inc., a middle-market electronics manufacturing firm. PACE

Acknowledgments

was the first Consortia company to be independently certified as "world-class." After spending years fine-tuning a state-of-the-art ERP system, Christy never hesitated to embrace Lean methodologies and led the way to virtually unplugging the MRP system and using an on-line pull system linked directly to the supply chain. Christy was an ongoing source of critical insight. John Walter eagerly embraced shop-floor financial metric boards and was instrumental in changing virtually every shop-floor practice in the pursuit of one-piece flow. Tom worked with Christy and our external auditors, PriceWaterhouseCoopers, to insure that a much simplified accounting system would not only provide more timely and actionable information, but would also meet the requirements of GAAP reporting.

This book, in its format, would never have materialized without the tutelage of Harvey Teres, who teaches English at Syracuse University. I'm sure teaching a finance and accounting practitioner the finer points of writing a novel was a much tougher task than his normal assignments of exposing wide-eyed freshmen to the literary classics, but he made the task enjoyable and kept me on the straight and narrow.

Thank you to my sisters, Judy Levy and Elyse Press, and to my parents, Iris and Bob, who served as sounding boards for many of my ideas and inspired me to continue when the going got tough.

And of course, special thanks to my very patient and loving wife, Sheila, who learned more than she could ever imagine about Lean techniques. No long-distance drive passed without her listening to me read the latest chapters of the book while anxiously awaiting her insightful comments. She was a constant source of encouragement and without her assistance this book would not have been possible.

Introduction

Tired of poor customer service, bloated inventories, quality problems, insufficient data for decision making, complex and expensive systems, and a never-ending stream of requests for capital equipment? It doesn't have to be that way. Much has been written about Lean, or world-class manufacturing, but we need more than an emphasis on changing the paradigm on the shop floor to be successful. There needs to be a radical change in all areas—including accounting—to achieve world-class results. Over the years I've heard too many stories about how the Lean journey came to a screeching halt because the executive suite didn't understand the financial implications of Lean. We need to develop a bond between the accountants and the manufacturing folks. We need to teach accountants how to actually improve results, not just be historians. And we need to simplify our processes before they strangle us.

I was one of those newly minted financial analysts from a top MBA school who could bring a project to its knees if the numbers weren't just right, even though I hadn't spent a day on the manufacturing floor. The numbers told the story, or so I thought.

In 1986, while I was Chief Financial Officer of Vermont Castings, I was asked to assume the additional role of Vice President of Manufacturing for this heavy industrial company. As the months passed, I became increasingly frustrated by the output of my own financial organization. The accounting reports provided absolutely no guidance on how to improve operational results. On the contrary, the accounting reports often promoted dysfunctional behavior. During the next fifteen years, as either Chief Financial Officer or Vice President of Manufacturing for a number of different companies, I relentlessly simplified the accounting reports until they assisted the shop-floor personnel in their quest to achieve superior results. And believe me, the shop floor always out-performed my expectations.

Never in my wildest dreams did I consider writing a novel, especially about accounting. Having spent my entire career at North American manufacturing companies, I always have been deeply concerned about our ability to compete globally without a radical change in thinking, particularly in accounting and finance. Until a few years ago, I never thought I could fully express how complete that change must be. Like many business people, I learned my lessons from textbooks, articles, training classes, mentors, and on-the-job training. When I finally realized that change isn't about numbers and analysis, so much as about hearts and minds, I turned to the genre that, more than any other, traffics in hearts and minds—the novel. The novel humanizes the problems, illustrates the gut-wrenching decisions that have to be made, and provides a perspective not possible in textbooks.

Who's Counting is a business novel that, for the first time, explains how accounting and manufacturing personnel must develop a partnership to successfully achieve world-class results. *Who's Counting* exposes the financial surprises that surface during a successful Lean journey and provides a road map to bring accounting practices into the twenty-first century.

World-class results are achievable on any continent, but only if we are world-class throughout our entire organization. Let's not rely on seventy-year-old accounting practices to compete in today's global market.

Table of Contents

Tricor Organizational Chart

Joe Reynolds
Member of Board of Directors, Tricor

Peter Worthington
President & CEO

Fred Chapman
Chief Financial Officer

Tom Hilton
Controller

Mary Simpson
Cost Accounting Manager

Scott Faulkner
General Accounting Manager

Howard Lee
Manager of Financial Analysis

Christy Kimball
Director of Information Technology

Mike Rogers
Vice President of Manufacturing

Jim Lawton
Plant Manager

Charles Gilbert
Director of Manufacturing Engineering

Debbie Johnson
Purchasing Manager

Tim Marx
Materials Manager

John Winters
Supervisor, Sheet Metal Shop

Randy Larsen
Director of Research & Development

Steve Taylor
Vice President of Sales & Marketing

Georgene Roberts
Manager of Customer Service

Tracy
Lean Champion, Philadelphia World Class Company

Tricor Selected Financial Data

Income Statement

Annual Sales		$ 300,000,000
Cost of Sales		
Material	$ 107,000,000	
Overhead	$ 33,000,000	
Direct Labor	$ 25,000,000	
Total Cost of Sales		$ 165,000,000
Gross Margin		$ 135,000,000
Operating Expenses		$ 111,000,000
Operating Income		$ 24,000,000
Taxes		$ 9,000,000
Net Income		$ 15,000,000

Other Financial Data

Accounts Receivable	$ 42,000,000
Days Sales Outstanding-Days	50
Average Inventory	$ 41,000,000
Fixed Costs in Inventory	$ 8,250,000
Inventory Turns	4
Shares Outstanding	250,000,000
Price/Earnings Ratio	15

1 The Board Speaks

"It got a little ugly in there," said Fred as he adjusted his seat.

"That's for sure," said Peter. "It's a hell of a way to tell me my honeymoon's officially over. We increased sales for the first time in six years and the Board blew me off. What the hell did they hire me for?"

"I know."

"I told them it would take two to three years to turn the company around, but that was before this damn recession hit. It's killing everyone."

The rain pelted the windshield and Peter struggled to follow the tail lights of the car in front of him. His S500 Mercedes had every safety feature imaginable, but the wipers couldn't keep up with the storm. The one-hour drive from the Board of Director's meeting in Boston to Tricor Electronics' corporate offices took an extra thirty minutes, enough time for Peter to rehash the board meeting with Fred, Tricor's Chief Financial Officer.

"When the Board recruited me two years ago, we agreed my priority was sales growth," continued Peter.

"They made that clear," acknowledged Fred.

"Earnings growth will follow. The Balance Sheet is strong enough to give us time to engineer a turnaround. That's what was so attractive about joining the company. I don't have to be a hatchet man."

"Joe never bought into that plan. He thinks you're way behind schedule."

"Joe's a pain in the ass."

"He doesn't care about sales growth, he's only interested in earnings."

Joe Reynolds was the manufacturing expert on the Board. He didn't support Peter's candidacy during the recruiting process and was a thorn in Peter's side from the outset.

"I'm getting sick of Joe's antics," said Peter. "That jerk spends the entire meeting stuffing his face with danish, waiting to criticize my performance."

Fred laughed. "Yeah, he's really putting on the pounds. But some of the other Board members are starting to agree with him."

"I know," said Peter as he grabbed the steering wheel with both hands and focused his attention on passing an eighteen wheeler.

"It's a good thing you listened to his advice."

"What?"

Fred repeated his comment. "At least you shut him up by following his advice."

"You can't shut Joe up, you just put him off a little bit. And I didn't hire Mike to appease Joe. That's not my style."

"I was wondering about that. Do you really think Mike will help us?"

"Absolutely. I hate to admit it, but Joe's right, we need help in manufacturing."

"What changed your mind?"

"When Joe first suggested hiring a Lean expert, I resisted. I had no idea what he was talking about. My background is in sales and marketing. Now I wonder if I should've hired someone much sooner."

Wow, Peter's second-guessing himself, thought Fred. "You had your hands full focusing on sales."

"Thanks, but that's just an excuse. That's my comfort zone."

"I'm serious, you had to stop the bleeding first. You've done a hell of a job bolstering the sales force and strengthening distributor relations. That's why sales are growing for the first time in years."

"Maybe so, but it's time to fix our other problems. The charts at the meeting showed earnings are suffering because of our high cost structure, pitiful service levels, and weak working capital management, particularly inventory turns."

Fred grimaced at the last item—working capital management. He thought it was an unwarranted attack on his area. How the hell could he lower accounts receivable with so many screwed-up orders? Customers refused to pay until backorders were cleared up. And regardless of inventory levels, the company never had the right product. "If we don't straighten out our internal problems, working capital will never get any better."

"I'm not blaming you. It's a company issue."

Fred took a deep breath and settled back in his seat. "I'm glad you realize that."

"Of course I do. We're one of the few North American manufacturers left in our niche of the electronics business..."

"And we should excel at customer service because of our domestic manufacturing base, but we're awful! We're growing sales in spite of our lousy service. I don't understand how offshore competition can have better service levels than we do. We have plants right here!"

"I'm starting to understand it."

"Really?"

"I didn't understand what Joe was talking about, so I attended a Lean Enterprise conference. Lean's supposed to take care of all those problems by streamlining production."

"There's been a million programs claiming the

same thing."

"That's what I thought. So I visited a number of 'Lean' companies and attended some Lean workshops."

"Were they any good?"

"Some of the results were unbelievable."

"Like what?"

"Huge improvements in customer service while slashing inventory, and productivity gains over fifty percent."

"Get outta here. Even if it were true, it'd be impossible to implement?"

"We'll find out. That's what Mike's here to do."

So far Mike's been a real jerk, thought Fred. Better not get into that discussion now.

"Do you mind if I stop for coffee?" asked Peter.

"I could use one too."

They pulled into the rest area, parked, and ran into the restaurant. The rain was coming down in sheets and Fred did his best to keep up with Peter's long strides, to no avail. They used the restroom, got two coffees to go, and ran back to the car.

"You want me to drive?" asked Fred, hoping to get a chance to get behind the wheel of the Mercedes. He could afford a Mercedes but preferred to invest his money.

"I'm fine."

As Peter pulled back onto the highway, Fred commented, "You left me in the dust back there."

"Sorry about that."

"Can I ask you something personal?"

"Sure."

"How come you never played pro basketball? You were the man in college. I've heard the stories."

Peter laughed. "I was OK for Ivy League ball. I went to one tryout camp and realized I was in over my head. My dad steered me to business. It's just as competitive and I thrive on that. How about you? Did you always want to be an accountant?"

"I've enjoyed working with numbers since I was a kid."

"What do you mean?"

"I grew up in the Bronx and was a sports fanatic. Yankees, Giants, and Knicks—my holy trinity. Every morning I rushed to the kitchen table to beat my dad to the sports section. I couldn't wait to check the box scores to calculate the statistics of my favorite players."

"No kidding."

"I did the calculations in my head."

"Batting averages and stuff like that?"

"Sure. It was easy."

"When did you decide to become an accountant?"

"I went to City College and took an introductory course in accounting. That's when I realized I'd be doing this kind of work the rest of my life. I got an undergraduate and master's in accounting and three years later became a CPA."

"Any regrets?"

"Not at all, I love what I do."

"That's obvious," said Peter as he slowed down and exited the highway. "We'll be at the garage in a few minutes. I was hoping we'd have time to talk about Mike."

"What did you want to know?"

"How you two are getting along?"

Fred responded hesitantly, "We're not off to a good start."

"I was afraid of that. Let's get together tomorrow to discuss it."

"I have a meeting in the morning. How about three o'clock?"

"That's fine."

Peter pulled into Tricor's parking garage and dropped Fred off at his car. They both headed home for the evening.

2 Hello Mike

Two years ago, Tricor's Board of Directors recruited Peter Worthington, Tricor's President, after he successfully led two other firms to leadership positions in their industries. Peter's background was impeccable; he was the star athlete at Harvard and one of the most publicized sales executives in the telecommunications and electronics distribution business. With his six foot four well-trimmed frame, perpetual tan, charismatic personality, and exemplary performance record, Peter was exactly the type of executive the Board targeted to increase sales and earnings.

"C'mon in," said Peter as he glanced at his watch. "I didn't realize it was three o'clock already."

Fred walked over to the corner curio and examined some mementos from Peter's college basketball career. "You must've been a lot better than you let on last night."

"I was OK, just not good enough to go to the next level."

"Do you play in any of the rec leagues?"

"I wish, but with my schedule, it's impossible."

"That's too bad," said Fred as he headed over to the chair in front of Peter's desk.

Peter quickly stood up, gathered his papers, and gestured to the table on the far side of the office. "Let's sit over here."

I hate sitting at the table, thought Fred as he followed behind Peter. It's serious. So I don't like Mike. What's the big deal?

Mike Rogers was the typical hard-charging manufacturing executive who could care less about corporate politics or appearances. He was 43 years old, five feet nine, rail thin, and an avid jogger. He had a job to do and was in a hurry to implement sweeping changes. Mike joined Tricor because Peter promised him carte blanche to institute the changes necessary for a successful and rapid implementation of Lean.

"So what's the problem with Mike?" asked Peter.
"I don't like him," responded Fred.
"Why?"
"We've had lots of manufacturing executives and no one ever had a problem with accounting or IT."
"Does Mike?"
"You bet. He thinks we've been operating in the dark ages."
"He said that?" said Peter jotting down some notes.
"Not exactly, but he implied it."
"What do you mean? He's only been with us for a month. Why would he think that?"
"I have no idea. He thinks everything we do is waste, or as he calls it, muda."
"Didn't he explain muda means waste in Japanese, and Lean's all about eliminating waste."
"Yeah, he talked about that. Muda's his favorite word. That's all he ever says and everyone jokes about it. I cringe every time I hear it."
"Let it go. Have you had any problems with the financial reports?"
"No. If we did, you'd know about it."
"That's for sure. We can't afford to have any surprises, especially now that the Board's putting a lot of

pressure on us."

"We won't if we continue with our current accounting routines. Otherwise I can't guarantee it."

"What do you mean by that?"

"Mike wants to change everything. He told me the accounting system's useless to manufacturing, and he has no use for the material requirements planning (MRP) system. You know how hard we worked to bring the system on line. We busted our butts for two years. He's really pissing everyone off."

"We'll have to make some changes, but it can't be that bad. He knows what he's doing."

"That's a big assumption," countered Fred as he leaned back in his chair and folded his arms. "Our auditors never found a problem with our work. In fact, they've always said we were doing a great job, particularly in cost accounting. We shouldn't just go change everything."

"You're jumping to conclusions. I doubt Mike's asking you to change everything. He's a little rough around the edges but, based on his references, he'll help us survive in this market."

"I wish I could agree but, based on what I've seen, I'm not convinced."

"I am. He's the right guy for the job. Our customer service stinks. We have more than enough inventory but we never have the right parts. And despite the productivity improvements, our margins are declining because we can't raise prices. He's dealt with these problems before."

"I know it's not a pretty picture..."

"Damn right it isn't. We're in a bind. We can't rely on the same old techniques. Mike's a top-notch manufacturing executive and he's familiar with the latest methods. If we have to make changes, so be it."

"I'm just not comfortable with him," said Fred.

"Give him time."

"I'll do my best to support him."

"That's not good enough. I'm counting on your complete support. We interviewed plenty of candidates and he was head and shoulders above the rest. I'm sorry you didn't get to meet him first, but we had to move on this."

"I'm probably jumping to conclusions."

"That's for sure," said Peter as he slowly got up from his chair. "We're beginning a challenging journey, and now, more than ever, we have to work as a team."

Just what I need before I retire, Fred thought. Why couldn't this Lean journey crap come along in three years?

Fred picked up his notepad and headed back to his office.

Fred Chapman loved his job at Tricor Electronics, but everything changed once Mike, the new Manufacturing Vice President, came aboard. Fred was Tricor's Chief Financial Officer for the past twenty years and spent his entire business career at the company after completing a five-year stint at a Big 5 accounting firm. He was 59 years old, well respected in the local financial community, and was looking forward to a part-time teaching position at the local business school upon his retirement in three years.

Fred spent the last five years fine-tuning all the accounting processes and led the effort to install a state-of-the-art computer system. For the past two years, he trained and coached the Controller and the Director of Information Technology (IT). They were handpicked because of their knowledge of the new systems and their experience working in the manufacturing sector.

Upon arriving home that evening, Fred's wife, Sheila, greeted him. Sheila and Fred recently celebrated their thirty-fifth wedding anniversary by spending two weeks in Hawaii. They had a wonderful time and looked forward to travelling in retirement.

Sheila had the patience of a saint, having taught Special Education at the elementary school level for the past twenty years. The stress of work took its toll, and she also looked forward to retiring in three years. She was ready for a break from the hardships she dealt with on a daily basis working with her students, all of whom were either mentally or physically handicapped.

Fred came in through the garage, dropped his briefcase in the corner of the entryway, and walked right by Sheila. He ignored the pile of mail waiting for him on the edge of the table.

"What's wrong?" Sheila inquired.

"Nothing."

"You expect me to believe that? Since we got back from Hawaii you've gotten more irritable each day. What happened?"

"You know the new guy, Mike..."

"Yeah..."

"He's going to be trouble."

"Isn't he in charge of manufacturing?"

"Yep."

"So what does he have to do with your area?"

"That's precisely the point. I don't know. He wants me to change everything so he can accomplish his goals. It's so damn frustrating! Why do they have to hire some young hot shot that'll make my life miserable?"

"C'mon, you've only been working with the guy since we got back from Hawaii. Give it some time. Maybe he'll surprise you."

"I doubt it."

"You told me the company needs help in manufacturing. Besides, you're retiring in three years; it'll go by quickly."

"He'll make the next three years hell. I don't need the aggravation, especially now."

"You're overreacting."

"No I'm not."

"He's bound to make some mistakes until he understands the company better. Didn't you say he was very successful at his other companies?"

"That's what everyone says, but you never know the real story."

"Peter wouldn't hire someone at that level without doing his homework."

"He's done a good job bringing in talent, but he blew this one."

"It doesn't matter. You have to support him until Peter realizes his mistake."

"I know. If Mike doesn't work out, Peter will get rid of him. He doesn't tolerate fools. In the meantime, I'll have to put up with him. I just hope his requests don't take too much time. After all, how different could his last company's accounting methods be from ours? Accounting is accounting."

Fred knew, despite his somewhat upbeat close with Sheila, Mike was going to be trouble. The fear of change at this stage of his career was upsetting. Fred regretted not spending more time at conferences, learning about the latest practices implemented at manufacturing firms.

3 Sales and Operations Planning

The next day Mike met with his Plant Manager, Jim Lawton, to prepare for Mike's first Sales and Operations Planning (S&OP) meeting. Jim was the typical manufacturing lieutenant and Mike liked him immediately. Jim got the job done no matter what, but he had to believe everyone was on the same page. He had no patience for politics and he detested meetings. He was a man of action and loved being on the plant floor.

S&OP was the monthly management meeting to balance market demand with production. The goal was to find an economical way to satisfy demand. If demand could not be met, then Tricor implemented programs to deal with shortfalls, such as extending lead-times, substituting products, outsourcing, overtime, and so forth. Similarly, if supply exceeded demand, the group discussed ways to cut back production or implement sales promotions to keep the plant and equipment fully utilized. From outward appearances, everyone was comfortable with the S&OP methodology.

Fred attended S&OP meetings to understand the impact of the production schedule on the financial statements. The Finance department used the S&OP data to project financial results for the upcoming quarter and the remainder of the year.

Each month the manufacturing group met in what was called the pre S&OP meeting to review the data and prepare alternatives for issues discussed at the

S&OP meeting.

Mike entered the manufacturing conference room for the pre S&OP meeting and noticed that Jim was standing in the back of the room, in heated discussion with one of the production planners.

"What's the matter, Jim?"

"I'll tell you what's the matter," responded Jim. "This S&OP process is a bunch of bullshit. I spend the entire meeting explaining that our lousy customer service levels are not manufacturing's fault."

"How bad are they?" Mike asked.

"Who the hell knows? It depends on whose numbers you look at. They change the measurements every month."

"C'mon, measurements aside, are we keeping up with the orders?"

"It's impossible."

"And they think it's your fault?"

"Are you kidding, of course they do! Especially the sales and marketing prima donnas. They don't listen to me. They think I'm making excuses. They keep telling Peter that our distributors are complaining because they don't get their orders on time. I know what they're really worried about is their freakin' sales commissions. It's like I'm taking money out of their pockets."

The production planners, schedulers and purchasing agents nodded in agreement.

"Will ya sit down and cool off," said Mike, glaring at Jim.

"How can I? Each month it gets worse and I'm sick of it."

"What does Peter think?"

"He sides with sales and marketing all the time."

"Doesn't he know you bust your butts just to achieve our current service levels."

Jim laughed, looked at his colleagues, then turned

toward Mike. "You're the new guy, and I don't want to be disloyal, but Peter really doesn't understand the problem. He's a Haavaad guy. He doesn't know shit about manufacturing."

"That's enough. Sit down and tell me what you mean."

"OK boss. Peter doesn't realize when we leave the S&OP meeting he's essentially approved a multimillion-dollar purchase order for parts. Our job is to execute the plan per S&OP and, damn it, we do a good job!"

"So your're saying you don't believe the forecast and the resulting parts requirements."

"Isn't he the bright one?" bellowed Jim to his captive audience. "I'll let you in on another little secret—not only is the forecast a joke, I don't use it. If we produced to the forecast you wouldn't be able to fit all of the crap in the building. Eventually we'd wind up throwing a lot of it out. It'd be obsolete and..."

"Does everyone feel the same way as Jim?" asked Mike.

"We sure do," responded one of the production planners.

Jim continued, "We miss the freakin' forecast three months in a row and sales and marketing still holds to the full year forecast. It doesn't make sense, but I don't know what to do about it. You're the big shot. I hope you can help because we're tired of it."

Everyone looked at Mike and waited for his response. "I understand. Unless the S&OP forecast is fairly accurate, you need to constantly change schedules and priorities."

"You bet."

Mike continued, "A lousy forecast combined with batch production is a recipe for failure. You guys must go in full expedite mode after each S&OP meeting."

"That's all we do all month."

"The problem you are describing is typical of most companies that drive their MRP systems from a forecast. MRP provides new information each week, but I bet you can't even keep up with the reports."

"Of course we can't. It's hopeless."

"Production planning based on forecasts is simply gambling. Forecasts are never, ever accurate. It'll never result in high customer service levels unless we fill the place with inventory, and even that might not work."

"So what the heck can we do about it? I don't know how much longer I can take this bullshit!"

"I'll explain at the S&OP meeting tomorrow."

"Why not now?"

"I'd rather go through it just once. I know it's not your nature, but be patient."

The S&OP meeting was held the second Wednesday of each month so that the latest financial results could be reviewed. The meeting was held in the austere Board Room where the presenters could take advantage of the latest technical innovations. One wouldn't expect any less of a 21st-century electronics company.

Peter, seated at the head of the twenty-foot long solid cherry conference table, opened the meeting with a crisp PowerPoint presentation about overall industry conditions and progress on major projects. Then he went around the table and everyone delivered their monthly reports. Steve Taylor, Vice President of Sales and Marketing, went first and reviewed the order pace for the current month and the most recent three-month period. Then he presented the forecast for the fourth quarter and the first half of the following year. Randy Larsen, Director of Research and Development, followed Steve and provided an update on new product development. Fred then reviewed the year-to-date financial performance and the revised full-year forecast. If Fred's numbers met or exceeded the original plan, the meeting was usually cordial. If Tricor wasn't meeting its commitment to the Board and Wall Street, the tension in the room was elevated a notch or two. Finally, Jim reviewed inventory levels by product and the production plan required to achieve Steve's sales projections.

"Jim," Steve said, "How come we have an eight-week backlog on our leading product? Our distributors are complaining that their advertising's finally working but they don't have anything to sell. They'll pull the advertising if we don't start shipping product. What are you going to do?"

"Damn it, Steve," said Jim as his face turned red and the veins in his neck started to bulge. "We go through this every few months. Every product line's over or under forecast by twenty to fifty percent. What do you expect?"

"I do the best I can," responded Steve as he turned the pages of the handout and tried to ignore Jim.

"I'm not a magician," said Jim as he pulled a pen from his pocket protector and made some quick notes. "We produce to the forecast and adjust as best as possible. You haven't hit the sales forecast for months. You're lucky we hedged the production plan. If we hadn't stopped producing some slow movers a couple of weeks ago our warehouse would be bursting. We can't keep jerking our suppliers around..."

"How about the line of surge protectors? We ran out of those," countered Steve.

"You beat the forecast and we didn't have enough parts to produce any more. Fred put a limit on purchasing..."

"Our line of credit is close to the limit. We can't afford any more inventory," said Fred.

Steve responded. "If we can't service our customers, we'll never make the sales numbers. How will that help our cash position?"

Jim ignored Steve and continued. "Randy's projecting that the new products will be released in two months. What should I do? Produce more of the products we overforecast and watch them build up in inventory, ramp up on today's hot product and hope they remain hot, or reserve capacity for the new product launch? I can't do it all. You tell me."

Peter had enough. He turned toward Mike, "What do you think?"

Mike quickly got up and walked to the front of the room. "You're all trying to achieve the same objectives, but it'll never work economically if you can't accurately forecast the marketplace. And I've met very few people who can do that in this or any business." He picked up a marker and wrote the word FORECAST on the whiteboard and then put a big X over it.

"What do you mean?" asked Randy.

"We spend so much time updating the forecast and we still can't get it right. Jim doesn't even use the information for production planning. If he did, we'd have even more inventory. I bet Fred doesn't even use the data for the financial forecast."

Fred couldn't help but smile at the comment. "Now that you mention it, I don't really use the actual numbers from the S&OP meeting. I check the sales forecast against historical patterns and overall market conditions and develop my own financial outlook."

"I thought that might be the case. Why don't you use the S&OP numbers?"

"It's too risky. There's too much at stake. I check everything against historical patterns and develop my own conservative outlook."

"I can't believe that," said Jim, staring at Fred. That's exactly what I do. I look at historical performance and massage the sales forecast to keep us out of trouble. If I didn't you wouldn't have enough space to store everything."

"Let me summarize what's going on," said Mike. "Steve admits he can't accurately forecast sales. Jim and his folks have little faith in the forecast and do their own plan. Fred has his own methods for the financial outlook. And Customer Service gets bombarded with calls from distributors because our order fill rate is terrible."

Peter leaned forward and looked at Mike. "What do you suggest?"

"Mike pointed at the whiteboard. "We stop forecasting demand and implement Lean philosophies ASAP."

"What the hell does that mean?" asked Steve.

"It means, among other things, we'll build product *only to* customer demand. That's the only way we'll reduce inventories, improve customer service, and eliminate the muda associated with forecasting, expediting, scheduling, and all that garbage."

"Eliminate the what?" responded Steve.

"Muda," said Mike. "It means waste. I explained it at the class last week but you missed it."

"I can't sell if I stay in the office."

"I know. We'll have a make up class."

"How can we improve customer service with lower inventories?" asked Fred. "How can we wait to build product until we have an order? Customer service will tank. It doesn't make sense."

"I know it sounds unreasonable, but trust me, it works. You'll have to think about business in an entirely different fashion, in a way none of you are used to thinking."

Fred responded, "C'mon now, we didn't just fall off the turnip truck. We've all been managing businesses for ten, twenty, or thirty years now. You've been here about a month and you're telling us we have to change everything. It's crazy!"

"I'd love to improve customer service, but Fred's

right," said Steve. "Reducing inventory scares the hell out of me. The distributors will be up in arms."

"I didn't say we could do it over night. It'll require a sustained effort from all of you over the next few years."

"Mike, from what I've heard, it sounds like you want to change everything in accounting right away," noted Fred.

"I want to get going, that's for sure. We'll have to change information systems and accounting methods, but we'll do it in stages. And Peter, I'll need your help most of all. You'll have to provide the leadership to stay the course if we're going to be successful in the long run. Without your commitment, we shouldn't even try to adopt Lean techniques."

"I understand. That's why you're here. But it's a lot to swallow for those in the room hearing this for the first time. It's so counterintuitive. But we have no choice."

"Not if we want to survive as a manufacturer. I've already started some new methods in the plant and soon I'll be meeting with suppliers to discuss different ordering procedures. I'll need your help soon, Fred. It'll be hard to move forward without the support of accounting and IT."

Steve couldn't wait to poke fun at his long-time associate, Fred. "I guess you'll be the guinea pig for this project."

"It's not a project," said Mike emphatically. "It's a permanent change in the way we do business." Mike turned toward Fred and continued, "So, Fred, can I count on your support?"

That asshole's putting me on the spot in front of everyone, thought Fred. And Peter's waiting to see what I say. Fred shifted in his chair and responded as enthusiastically as he could. "Sure, just let me know what you need."

"Great, we'll have to make some reporting changes, but don't worry."

Peter emphasized the importance of Fred's role. "Lean won't work without your support, Fred. From what I've heard, accounting's often the biggest impediment to a successful Lean journey. I know you won't let that happen here."

"Of course not."

"One last thing, Mike," said Peter. "Is the S&OP process a waste of time?"

"No. It'll continue to play a critical role, just in an entirely different way."

"Good, because despite its flaws, we accomplish a great deal at these meetings."

"So what do we have to change?" asked Steve.

"Eventually we won't need to forecast items at the detail level."

"Wow, that's music to my ears. I can't wait."

"I bet you can't," said Jim. "I don't know why you bother to forecast anything now. It's useless."

Mike stared at Jim and he shut up.

Mike continued. "In a Lean environment, manufacturing focuses on the exceptions—unusual orders you might be working on, the timing of new product introductions, things like that. We'll use the meeting to discuss activities outside the norm so we can adjust capacity over the long term."

"So the exact details of the short-term forecast aren't that important?" asked Randy.

"Once we get going, it won't matter what specific products we sell, as long as the mix doesn't vary too widely. We'll develop techniques that allow us to respond to customer requirements rapidly. That's the beauty of Lean. But it'll take time to get there, so let's not change the format yet. We've got a lot of work to do in manufacturing first."

"So when exactly do you need my help?" asked

Fred.

"Throughout the journey, starting immediately."

"Let me know what I have to do. But I don't understand why accounting and IT have to change."

"We'll go over that separately."

"Thanks Mike." Peter went over the remaining agenda items and adjourned the meeting.

Fred, Steve, and Randy walked down the hallway together and congregated outside Steve's office.

"Mike has all the answers," said Steve. "I have to hand it to those manufacturing guys, they always have a new program to solve our problems. We've gone from quality circles to statistical process control to teams and nothing's really changed."

"At least none of those programs interfered with my departments," said Fred.

"It's going to be fun watching you deal with it." said Randy."

"Thanks a lot. I can't wait until Mike gets involved in R & D. Then we'll see how you like it."

"Not a chance," responded Randy as they headed toward their offices.

It'd be great to eliminate the crap that goes on at each S&OP meeting, thought Fred, but how the hell can accounting and IT solve the problems. And Peter must be feeling pretty good, but he better watch out. Mike makes it sound too easy. It's never that easy.

Jim followed Mike back to his office. "So, boss, what did ya think?"

"It's gonna be tough," responded Mike as he collapsed into his chair. "I don't know if I can go through the agonizing start-up ritual one more time. I've gotta teach everyone to think differently."

"Is it that tough?"

"Not for manufacturing. I hope you don't mind my saying this, but you guys are used to following orders. Hell, you've probably been through so many programs over the years, this doesn't seem like a big deal."

"Ain't that the truth, boss. But none of them ever worked."

"Lean's different. Once the plant experiences some initial successes, they'll give Lean a chance. But it won't be easy. They'll be waiting for us to fail."

"Hey, I'm not convinced. I don't understand any of it yet. You gotta prove this shit works. If it does, I'll take care of the plant."

"I'm not worried about convincing you. It's the admin areas that are the problem. The benefits aren't as tangible and the managers are much more protective of their 'turf.'"

"They're a bunch of wussies. This Lean shit will be worth it just to see you straighten out their areas. It's about time."

Mike picked up the phone. He covered the receiver with one hand and whispered to Jim, "It's Peter."

"You want me to leave?" asked Jim as he started to head for the door.

Mike motioned to him to sit down.

"I know it's all new for them. I'll run a series of classes. Don't worry about it.

"Yeah.

"Yeah.

"I'll spend some extra time with Fred. I know he's a good friend of yours.

"You're right, it's a shock to the accountants. Don't worry, you can count on it.

"Talk to you later."

"Fred and Peter are pretty close you know," said Jim.

"Yeah, Peter's worried about him. Lean's a tough sell for the financial people. They're so set in their ways."

"No shit. I gotta go make some product. See ya."

4 Tricor

Tricor was a middle market company that went public eight years ago and experienced tremendous success in the first few years. Four years ago, earnings growth stalled as new competitors entered the market and exerted tremendous pricing pressure. The stock nose-dived and only recently began to recover due to Peter's success in growing revenue. Investors now were clamoring for commensurate growth in earnings per share and cash flow.

Tricor had about one thousand employees spread among two facilities in North America and one facility in Europe. Sales offices were located throughout the world. The largest manufacturing facility was co-located with corporate headquarters in New England. Since most manufacturing took place at the corporate headquarters site, Fred and his staff were heavily involved in manufacturing operations.

Tricor completed its budget proposal forty-five days prior to year-end to allow time for Board of Director approval, comments, and revisions. With only three months until the new fiscal year, Fred felt the pressure to wrap things up.

Mary Simpson, the Cost Accounting Manager, was a key player in the Accounting department. Mary joined Tricor two years ago and was a breath of fresh air. The new computer system was great, but there was so much detail embedded in the cost reports that it was virtually impossible to understand anything, especially since Mary's predecessor hadn't set up any of the reporting routines correctly. Mary spent her first year straightening out the cost reports and, in the process, eliminated the month-end surprises that occasionally surfaced.

Mary just passed her CPA exam and wanted to expand her horizons by moving out of cost accounting and into general accounting. She wanted a Controllership position at one of Tricor's subsidiaries, but needed more experience in general accounting. She looked forward to completing the budget and then moving into a new position. Fred promised to broaden her experience as part of her career development.

Fred turned to Mary at the staff meeting. "We're reviewing the manufacturing budget with Mike next week and I want to make sure we're ready."

"Don't worry, I'm almost done."

"Good. Mike has his own ideas of how a manufacturing budget should be put together. He's probably been disappointed by cost accounting at his prior companies, so let's show him we're different. If you have any questions, see me."

"I've heard some of the rumblings about Mike already," said Mary.

"Really? What've you heard?," inquired Fred as he rubbed his beard, leaned forward, and stared intently at Mary.

"You know I have a good relationship with Jim. Well, I don't know if I should say this..."

"Go ahead," urged Fred.

"Well, he told me I better strap on my seat belt."

"What did he mean by that?" shouted Fred.

"He said Mike has some wild ideas about tracking costs in the plant. He even told me he was in Mike's office and overhead him talking to the Controller of his last company."

"What did he say?"

"Mike told the Controller he was going to have to redo the entire costing system just like he had done twice before."

"You're kidding?"

"I wish. And that's not all. He said he didn't understand why accounting hadn't changed in decades, and he was tired of fixing accounting as well as manufacturing."

"I can't believe he said that. Who the hell does he think he is? He's only been here a short time and he thinks he has all the answers."

"It seems that way. Even Jim was surprised by Mike's comments."

"How come Jim told you all of this?"

"He wanted to give me a heads up so I could be ready for Mike. I've helped Jim out with a few things, so he was just returning the favor."

"I don't care what Mike thinks; we've nothing to be worried about. But, just to make sure, review the cost allocation routines prior to meeting with Mike. Make sure everything's up to date."

"Not a problem," responded Mary.

"Also, check with manufacturing engineering to make sure the labor standards have been updated."

"OK, but you know that's part of the normal process."

"Yeah, I know. I just don't want to miss anything. How about purchasing? Have they entered the new standards into the system?"

"We've taken care of everything, quit worrying," said Mary. "The manufacturing budget's under control."

"You're right. I want to show him that we're on top of everything."

"Hey, I've done manufacturing budgets at many companies, and our system's the best."

"Thanks."

"You're welcome."

"One more thing. Have you completed the departmental statements yet?"

"They'll be done tomorrow."

"Good. How many manufacturing departments do we track now?"

"Seventeen."

"That'll make it easy for Mike to monitor activity in the plant. I bet he didn't have that level of detail at his last company. I don't see what he can object to."

"I'm with you. This is the best shape we've been in since we installed the new system. It took awhile to work out the bugs, but it's a smooth process now. Mike will be impressed."

Christy Kimball was Tricor's Director of Information Technology. During the last two years, she worked wonders on the system. She spent much of her time supporting manufacturing because of its endless requests for custom reports. Christy, one of the youngest members of the team, was tech savvy, and had a knack for solving complex business issues with simple systems solutions.

Fred turned to Christy. "How we doing with the computer support for manufacturing?"

"We provided Jim with just about everything he asked for. The work order system's working well, the routings have been corrected, and Mary's proved out all the feeds to the general ledger."

"Great. We're in good shape for the meeting next week. Why don't you join us in case Mike questions any of the IT stuff."

"No problem," responded Christy.

"Thanks for your support," Fred said, wrapping up the meeting. He went to his office to try and figure out what, if anything, he could have overlooked, and concluded everything was in order. He was ready for anything Mike would throw at him, or so he thought.

5 The War

Tricor's budgeting process was perfected over the last five years. The manufacturing portion of the budget was the most complex as it involved the most departments, employees, and dollars, had a variety of complex cost variance projections, and required a full updating of the standard cost for each item. The manufacturing budget took a couple of iterations to complete and there was no slack in the schedule to absorb any delays.

Fred, Mary, Christy, and Mike gathered in the Board Room to review the first pass of the manufacturing budget. Accounting prepared a preliminary budget to assist Mike, and had forwarded it to him two weeks ago for his review. Fred wanted the budget completed on time and had taken this precautionary step. The budget schedule would not be achieved if everyone waited for Mike to get up to speed.

Joining Mike were Jim, Charles Gilbert, the Director of Manufacturing Engineering, Tim Marx, the Materials Manager, and Debbie Johnson, the Purchasing Manager.

The manufacturing staff were seated on one side of the table while Fred and his staff were seated on the opposite side. Fred passed out an agenda, which Mike quickly scanned and set aside.

"How about going over the departmental spending

first, then the projected variances, capital spending, and inventory projections, and then review next year's standard costs?" asked Fred.

"Before we start a detailed review, tell me how you calculate product costs," asked Mike. "I hope you don't use a full absorption cost accounting system."

"Of course we use full absorption."

"I was afraid of that."

"We've always done it that way."

"That doesn't mean a thing."

"I don't know what you expect, but it's not like we're the only company using full absorption. I network with a lot of CFOs and Controllers, and I've never come across anyone in manufacturing who doesn't use full absorption."

"Just because it's popular doesn't mean we should use it."

"Then how would we value inventory or properly record monthly results? We use some pretty sophisticated methods to make sure we allocate overhead properly to each product, so if you're worried about accuracy, we've taken care of that."

"With all due respect, I've no use for a full absorption accounting system. Your staff couldn't get it right if you doubled your efforts. No one could. And besides, it doesn't provide manufacturing with any useful information."

"How can you say that?" snapped Mary tapping her designer fingernails on the table. "When I came here the cost system was a mess. I've spent a lot of time fixing it. So don't say it's useless. That's bull!"

Fred was shocked. Usually Mary was subdued at meetings, but Mike hit a sensitive nerve by criticizing the cost system. That was Mary's baby.

"I agree," said Christy. "I've worked closely with Mary, debugging the system and making sure the manufacturing data's correctly fed to the financial systems.

We've checked all the reports and I can assure you that the information's correct. We don't have the largest staff in the world, but our technical know-how is top notch."

"I'm not questioning your systems, ability, or commitment to provide accurate data for the manufacturing organization."

"So what's your problem?" shot back Christy.

"The cost system doesn't support a Lean manufacturing approach, and for the most part it's muda."

Fred slammed his coffee mug on the table. "Damn it, don't call our efforts waste!"

"Take it easy. I'm not trying to offend anyone. I'm just trying to tell you what I'll need."

"Take it easy! Who are you kidding? You've been criticizing accounting since you got here."

"I'm just trying to explain that the cost system will have to change."

"You're not doing a very good job at it. I know you want to improve manufacturing, but don't expect our help if you treat us like this. If you want to discuss the budgets, I'll continue; otherwise we're leaving." Fred gathered his papers and started to get up.

"Hey, I'm sorry. Please, sit down."

Fred refused and stood by his chair.

"I just can't stand to beat around the bush. It's muda."

"It's arrogant," responded Fred.

"I'm really sorry. C'mon, sit down and let me start over."

"Why, what's going to change?"

"Let's try a different approach."

"Like what?"

"Forget the budget discussion. Let me ask you a few questions, give you some time to get the answers, and then let's all get back together to discuss it. Can we try that?"

"Are you kidding?" said Fred as he started to head

34

out of the room. I came here to review the manufacturing budget, not take a quiz."

"Hold on a second. It's really important to go over the questions. It won't take long and I guarantee you'll all learn a lot about Lean Accounting."

"We're on a tight schedule and can't afford to go on a wild goose chase." Everyone's waiting to see what I do, thought Fred. What in the hell is he up to now? Would it really be that easy to bring the two sides together by answering a few questions? "Let's hear the questions, then I'll decide."

Mike raced to the easel at the front of the room. He picked up the marker, paused to gather his thoughts, and began writing his questions on the flip chart.

"What's the percentage breakdown of cost of sales by material, labor and overhead?

"How accurate are the cost components?

"Are total product costs accurate because they're calculated to four decimal places?

"Estimate the costs incurred to maintain the labor reporting system.

"Estimate the costs incurred to maintain the allocation schemes for overhead.

"Graph the labor and overhead costs for the last 24 months. How much do they fluctuate relative to volume changes?"

"Are you almost done?" asked Fred.

"I'm listing everything. I want you to know exactly what's on my mind."

"It's about time, but I don't have all day."

"I'm almost finished. Then you can decide if you want to answer the questions."

"Go ahead," said Fred as he pulled his chair out, sat down and kept all of his folders on his lap.

"Why are there so many individual departments in manufacturing?

"What's the benefit of providing detailed expense

reporting on wages and benefits for each department?"

"What do you mean?" asked Scott.

"Separate line items for payroll taxes, vacation, holiday, and pension expenses.

"What percentage of each manufacturing supervisor's individual departmental expense is truly under the supervisor's control?

"What are the company's operating expenses, and to what extent are they spread, or allocated, to individual product costs?"

Mike flipped the page over the back of the easel and continued.

"In addition to the accounting issues, I have the following philosophical questions."

Fred interrupted, "First accounting, now philosophy. When does it end?"

"Give me five more minutes."

"Hurry up," Fred begrudgingly agreed.

"Ask the manufacturing staff how much they really use the accounting reports.

"Ask them if they really understand the variances and how to improve them.

"Ask the supervisors if the accounting reports let them know where labor was overspent or inefficient, when the variance occurred, or whether the variance was improving or deteriorating during the month.

"Let me know if the accounting reports indicate if customer orders were filled.

"Finally, do the reports tell my supervisors what to improve, do they identify waste, and do they identify obstacles to the continuous flow of product in the plant?" Mike put the marker down and returned to his seat.

"We don't have time for this nonsense."

"It's not nonsense. They're serious questions. I know you're busy with budgets, but this is critical if we're going to resolve our differences."

Fred turned to Mary and Christy. "Do you have time to work on this?"

Christy responded first. "It'll take time, but I'm curious to see the answers."

"I agree," said Mary. "It won't be too bad, as long as Jim, Charles, and Tim give us their support."

"Just tell us what you need," said Jim.

Charles and Tim also offered up their help.

"OK," said Fred. "But where are you going with this?"

"We need reporting that reflects what's happening on the plant floor, is understood by everyone, and will keep up with the changes we'll be making on a regular basis. And most importantly, we need your staff's time and brain power to assist with real improvements in the shop."

"Isn't that the job of the manufacturing group?" asked Fred.

"It's all our jobs," countered Mike.

"We can't take on additional responsibilities. You must be kidding."

"You won't have time if you use the same methods that've been in place for decades. That's the whole point. You'll have to eliminate some of the work."

"So you're saying we're wasting our time now?"

"Don't take it personally, Fred."

"What do you mean don't take it personally? You've done nothing but insult the department and now you're asking for our help. You're quite a politician."

"All I'm saying is there are better accounting methods than what you're using. Traditional accounting isn't consistent with Lean manufacturing, and we don't have the time or resources to do both."

"That's your opinion."

"You're right. But it's based on operating in both environments. Perhaps it'll help if I share my goals with all of you."

"That would be nice," said Fred sarcastically.

"I'd like to go to a material-only cost system, eliminate most of the departments, treat direct labor as a period cost, and calculate product costs at the family level."

"Wow, that's different," said Mary.

"It sure is. If you work through my questions, you'll understand why. Are there any other questions?"

"You've taken enough of our time. We'd like to support you, but you're asking for things we've never heard of, or seen in practice. A material only-cost system, eliminate most of the departments.... it's stupid."

"It's different, but what do you have to lose?"

"I have a budget to finish. We'll see what we can do."

"Thanks."

6 The Team Comes First

"C'mon in," said Peter as he motioned Fred into his office.

"I don't know how much more I can take of your new guy in manufacturing."

"Calm down."

"I can't."

"What's going on."

"Mike's wasting my time with a bunch of meaningless assignments."

"What did he ask you to do?"

"He wants me to answer all sorts of questions about manufacturing costs. And he wants to know if the financial reports show his supervisors how to improve results."

"That doesn't sound unreasonable coming from someone asked to approve a budget of tens of millions of dollars. What's the problem?"

"Maybe the questions aren't that bad, but who can hear them through all the insults? I'm telling you, the guy's a jerk."

"Don't you think you're blowing it out of proportion."

"No! I thought you did your homework on him. He's not a team player. I don't think I can work with him."

"I've never seen you like this. Mike's not even been here two months. How could he get you so upset?"

"I've never run into someone who is so arrogant."

"Let me talk with him and find out why he's coming on so strong. There must be something behind this. I'll get back to you before your next meeting with him."

"It isn't just me. He's insulting my staff. They don't like working overtime to answer his questions. They think he's a joke."

"He's not a joke, I'm sure of that. I'll talk to him tomorrow. In the meantime, do me a favor and start working on his request. If you don't think it's worth the effort you have my permission to stop. But give it an honest try first."

"If we're not getting anywhere, I'll stop. I'm not a fool." Fred eased himself out of the chair and headed for the door.

"Thanks," said Peter, as he walked over and gently put his hand on Fred's shoulder. "Don't make more out of this than is necessary. It'll work out just fine."

After Fred left, Peter thought about the conversation. He hadn't seen Fred so upset in quite awhile. Perhaps Fred's assessment was correct. If so, then Mike had duped both him and the Board. It didn't make sense, especially in light of the glowing recommendations Mike received. Peter asked his assistant to cancel his upcoming meeting and then dialed Mike's extension.

"Hello, Peter," Mike said as he glanced at the caller ID display.

"Would you come down to my office," responded Peter. "I have something I need to discuss with you."

"Sure, be right there."

Mike entered Peter's office and joined him at the table.

"What the heck's going on?" Peter asked.

Mike stiffened and hesitated a second. "What are you talking about?"

"I hired you because you're a Lean expert, but your people skills will stop the Lean journey dead in its tracks. What are you trying to do to Fred and his staff?"

"Take it easy. I've helped turn around three companies..."

"I'm not interested in what you did at the other companies, I'm interested in how you handle yourself here."

"Can I finish?" insisted Mike

"Go ahead."

"At my previous companies we had a hell of a time getting going because of the resistance of the administrative areas, particularly accounting and IT."

"That's no surprise, given the way you treat them."

"Believe me, I was very patient at my other companies."

"Like you are now?"

"I don't have the patience anymore to wait for everyone to change their ways. I know what's got to be done and I want to implement as fast as possible. Is that so terrible?"

"You know it is," said Peter as he slowly got up and peered out the window. He turned back toward Mike. "I can't believe I'm hearing this from you, the Lean expert. Didn't you tell me Lean's a 'people program' first and foremost? Didn't you say it was about a team effort?"

"Yeah, but..."

"Please, don't yeah but me. I've gone to all of the seminars, and if there's one thing I've learned, its Lean will never get off the ground with you're approach. We're implementing a cultural change and you'll need everyone's support, especially Fred's."

"I know."

"Well, you're not acting that way. This isn't a manufacturing program; it's Lean Enterprise we're talking about. It'll affect the entire company. Maybe I hired the wrong guy for the job."

"That's not the case."

Peter returned to his chair. "Your references said you were a team player. What's really going on here?"

"I've been implementing Lean for fifteen years now, and every time I start over, I'm less tolerant of traditional methods. How many times can I see the same idiotic things repeated at each new company and not get fed up with it? Everyone thinks they're doing a great job, but it's bullshit."

"Well, what do you expect? They're all well intentioned, hard working folks. But they don't understand Lean yet."

"Yeah, they're working hard, but nobody's working smart. It's a long journey and I want to get on with it. It's so frustrating!"

"More so for them. They're the ones whose world will be turned upside down. Do you expect them to change over night?"

"I wish that were possible."

"But it's not. That's why you have to be patient. You're supposed to be the Lean teacher. You told me Lean's about teamwork and continuous improvement, not about one hard charging son-of-a-bitch with a take-no-prisoners attitude."

"C'mon, I wasn't that bad."

"It sounds like you were. It doesn't mean a thing if you know exactly where you're going but aren't willing to train the rest of the company. You can't do it alone."

"I'm afraid it's going to go too slow with Fred. He's going to resist everything. He wants to coast until his retirement."

"That was uncalled for."

"It's true."

"Everyone's going to resist—that's natural. It's your job to convert them, not bully them."

"Maybe I was a little too aggressive, but we need results. I've seen the numbers."

"Sure, we need results. I know that better than anyone. But it's long-term results I'm after. I can't afford to have you alienate everyone. I'd rather retool now when we're just starting our journey."

Mike cleared his throat, took a deep breath and conceded, "I guess you're right."

"This isn't guesswork, I know I'm right," responded Peter adamantly."

"I've been doing Lean transformations so long, I was beginning to think I could do it all by myself."

"We both know that's not possible."

"I gotta confess, I'm still upset over the sale of my last company."

"Why?"

"I worked so hard to implement Lean and the new owners didn't support it. They didn't understand the concepts and the company will suffer. You either go forward or you slip back to traditional methods; there's no middle ground. We could've accomplished so much more."

"That won't happen here. Lean's part of our long-term strategy. Just do your part."

"I'll make amends with Fred and his folks. You can count on it."

"Let me give you some advice. Fred has a lot of influence at this company. Win him over and the journey will be a lot easier."

"I understand."

"Good. And remember that there's no compromising on the approach. We implement by the book. Don't disappoint me."

"I won't."

Peter stood up and extended his hand. Mike responded in kind, thanked Peter for the advice, and quickly exited the office.

Peter thought about the conversation. Based on everything he heard about Mike, his behavior at Tricor was totally out of character. Mike had spent five years with his last company and achieved tremendous results from his Lean initiatives before the company was acquired and he was summarily let go. The sale surprised Mike and affected him more than Peter realized. From his own experiences, Peter knew it was gut-wrenching for someone to see five years of steady progress end without having the satisfaction of seeing the journey through.

The thought of starting from scratch, combined with the knowledge of how long the Lean journey would take, was frustrating to Mike.

Peter understood Mike's impatience and was disappointed he hadn't anticipated it. He would discuss it with Fred the first thing the next morning.

As Mike headed back to his office he ran into Jim.

"What's the matter boss? You don't look too good."

"I just got my ass chewed out by Peter."

"He must've heard about the meeting. You really pissed everyone off. Mary was very upset."

"Yeah, I guess I was pushing too hard."

"I hope you don't mind my saying so, but you were a jerk. Fred, Mary, and everyone else work very hard to help us out. You acted as if they're incompetent."

"Was I really that bad?"

"Yep. I know Lean requires a different way of thinking, but you'll never accomplish anything with that approach. What did you expect to happen, boss?"

"I wasn't thinking."

"No shit. If you need the folks in accounting and IT to make Lean work, you have your work cut out for you."

"I know. I have to gain their confidence, and soon. I think I have an idea that might help."

"And what's that?"

"Do you remember the company I told you about

in Philly that's been practicing Lean for about ten years?"

"Yeah, I remember. What did you have in mind?"

"I joined the local manufacturing Consortia and they're taking a group to visit that company next Wednesday. I thought I'd take Mary with me so she'd get a much better understanding of Lean and her role in the journey. I need a Lean advocate in accounting and she'd be the ideal person. What do you think?"

"Why Mary?"

"A lot of the transformation takes place in the Cost Accounting area. If Mary's comfortable with the changes, it'll be easier to convince Fred."

"Maybe, but you better talk to Fred first and mend some fences."

"I know. I'll see if he'll go to lunch with me tomorrow."

"Good. I've been doing some reading on Lean and I'm ready for the challenge. I'd like to make sure you're here to help us with it."

"Don't worry, I'm not planning on going anywhere."

"I wasn't exactly thinking it would be your choice. I better get back to work now."

"I appreciate your honesty, Jim."

"Just doing my job, boss. See ya later."

7 Reconciliation

Fred and Mary were in the middle of a discussion when they heard a tap on the door. They were surprised to see Mike.

"I'm glad I caught up with both of you. I know you were pissed off at yesterday's meeting and I want to apologize for my behavior. I was a little out of line."

"Only a little?" Fred said with a smirk as he turned back toward Mary.

"I'm trying to apologize. Let's not get into another argument."

Fred snapped back, "I don't want that either. You were way out of line, and yes, it pissed me off."

"I said I'm sorry, and I mean it."

"Well, we'll see how you act from here on out. Apology accepted."

"How about you, Mary?"

"I'm willing to wipe the slate clean."

"Thanks. Now, can we start the process over? I really need your support."

"So that's what the apology's about— you need our help," said Fred.

"I'm apologizing for my behavior, not for wanting to move forward with the Lean transformation. You know that's why I was brought on board."

"Yeah, I know. I just don't understand it."

"It takes time. And it won't work without your help."

"You knew we weren't a Lean company, so what did you expect? We need some training and you need to be patient."

"You're right," conceded Mike. The idiot's making me squirm now and enjoying every minute of it.

"My staff's anxious and you only made matters worse yesterday. I'll support you, but we need to work together."

"I screwed up. I have an idea to get everyone on board."

"What?" asked Fred rolling his eyes.

"I'll be visiting a world class manufacturing company next week and I was wondering if Mary could join me. It'll be a great educational experience and she can share her findings with the department. What do you think?"

"Do you have time," Fred asked as he turned towards Mary.

"I can get away for the day, but that's not what I'm worried about," said Mary.

"You don't sound too good," responded Mike.

Mary continued in a raspy voice, "I've been feeling terrible the last few days. I have a doctor's appointment tomorrow. Plan on my going unless you hear otherwise. I hope I'll be better by then. Thanks for the invite."

"I hope you can make it."

Mike turned toward Fred.

"Can you join me for lunch and I'll explain Lean accounting to you? It'll help for our next meeting."

Fred hesitated before responding.

"Can't it wait?"

"Sure it can, but the sooner we discuss Lean, the better you'll understand what I'm trying to do."

"Do we have to meet for lunch? Can't we meet here?"

"My explanation will be more effective over

lunch."

"That doesn't make sense."

"You'll find out soon enough. C'mon, join me for lunch."

"Now I'm curious. You're treating, right?"

"You betcha."

"How about if I swing by your office at noon?"

"That'll work for me. See you then."

Mike left, and Mary and Fred stared at each other.

"Maybe he's not that bad," said Mary. "I like his idea of heading to Philadelphia. It'll be good to see another company that's been through a Lean transformation."

"I like the idea also," said Fred. I'm just not sure who the real Mike is. I hope it's the guy who was just in here."

"He seemed sincere."

"I agree. I just hope a pattern isn't developing."

"Me, too."

"Lunch should be interesting."

Mary laughed, "Yeah, I bet it will be. Let me know how it goes."

"Will do."

Right after Mary left, Fred received a phone call from Peter. "Fred, I had a chat with Mike and I understand where he's coming from. He feels bad about yesterday's meeting. I should've seen it coming and headed it off first. Don't blame Mike, blame me."

"I was wondering what happened."

"What do you mean?"

"Mike just left. He was very apologetic. We're going out to lunch to discuss Lean."

"Great!"

"Whatever you said to Mike, it worked. He was a different person. Maybe there won't be any more problems."

"There shouldn't be. He's just getting over some issues from his previous position. Give me a call if anything comes up."

"You can count on it."

8 Chinese Food and Lean

Mike drove Fred to the Mandarin House, the local Chinese restaurant jokingly referred to as the company cafeteria by Tricor employees. There was never a wait for a table, the service was impeccable, and the food was excellent.

"There are a lot of Tricor employees here," noted Mike as the hostess escorted them to their table.

"It's always packed with our employees. Haven't you eaten here before?" asked Fred.

"No. I don't like to take the time. I'd rather eat at my desk and get some work done."

"Me, too. But if I go out, this is usually the place."

"I hear it's really good."

"It is. They do a great job."

"But what if you want to have a serious business conversation?" asked Mike as he slid into a booth and took a menu from the hostess.

"If it's confidential, this is definitely not the place. But it works both ways."

"What do you mean?"

"If we get along, everyone will hear about it. So it can work to our advantage."

"Good. We know what we have to do then."

"So what did you want to talk about?" asked Fred.

"You're probably wondering how I could possibly have any idea about what needs to be done in accounting?"

"I sure am. You came on very strong yesterday and being a manufacturing guy, you confused and offended my staff and me."

"I didn't mean to offend you."

"You had a lot of nerve telling everyone how they should do their jobs. How do you know how we should report results? What do you know about accounting?"

"I guess it's your turn to ask the questions."

"It sure is. How do you like it?" said Fred sarcastically.

Mike ignored the comment and continued. "It'd clear things up if I explained my background a little better."

"That sure would help."

"I wasn't always a manufacturing guy."

"Really, I thought you've been doing this all your life."

"As a matter of fact, I'm more a finance person than a manufacturing expert."

"You're kidding," exclaimed Fred.

"I started out in finance and was fortunate to advance rapidly in a small, growth oriented, heavy manufacturing company. I became the Vice President of Finance five years later, when I was only 28 years old..."

"You, a VP of Finance? Now that's a surprise!"

"Why's that?"

"It's hard to imagine."

"You don't know me well enough yet. You might have a different opinion in a few months."

I sure hope so, thought Fred. "We'll see. Go ahead and finish explaining your background."

"Shortly after I became the VP of Finance, the company experienced the typical operational problems of coping with growth and the resulting complexity of the business. Our margins were declining, the product offering was expanding, inventories were out of control, and customer service levels were not competitive, even though we had the most up-to-date MRP system. We put a lot of effort into coming up with the best forecast possible, but if it was within thirty percent we were lucky."

"So what happened?"

"Our President asked me to head up the manufacturing organization."

"That's crazy. Why did he do that?"

"He realized we needed a radical change in our manufacturing strategy, and what seemed like a totally ridiculous decision at the time was, in hindsight, a brilliant move."

"I don't understand," said Fred as he emptied a Sweet and Low into his cup and reached for the teapot. "Tea?"

"Sure," replied Mike as he extended his cup. "Thanks."

"It was a brilliant move because we had to change our thought processes at a time when there weren't very many companies in North America practicing Lean methods. Since I wasn't wedded to any particular manufacturing strategy, I didn't have to reverse years of bad habits."

"But what did you know about manufacturing?"

"Not much. Before I started my new position, our President had the foresight to send me to Japan for three months to learn under a Lean master and see Lean in action."

"What was that like?"

"It was fascinating. It all seemed so logical, yet, when I came home, the manufacturing folks had a million reasons why it wouldn't work at our company."

"And you proved them wrong?"

"It wasn't easy. But our President knew I would embrace the new methods and, combined with my passion for process improvement, would bring along the rest of the group."

"So, how did your financial background come into play?" asked Fred, so engrossed in the conversation that he ignored the waitress standing near by. Mike signaled to her to come back later.

"That's the best part of the story. My financial background turned out to be a huge bonus, which I don't think our President anticipated."

"I don't understand."

"It didn't take long to realize that just about everything produced in the accounting area was of little or no use to manufacturing, and would be next to impossible to use in a Lean environment. So I had the dual task of implementing Lean Manufacturing and Lean Accounting."

"Sounds like a huge undertaking."

"It was. But if the accounting routines didn't change along with the manufacturing processes, we would've never succeeded. We made up the rules as we went, and since I had the full support of our President and our Controller, who still reported to me, it made my mission a lot easier."

"I imagine having the Controller report to you during the transition was critical."

"It helped very much because we were breaking new ground and a lot of experimentation was required. If a problem arose it was my responsibility, not the Controller's."

"Did you have any problems?"

"Are you kidding?" Mike said as he laughed out loud and took a sip of tea. "Of course we did, but we worked our way through them."

"How about at the other companies you worked for. Did finance and accounting report to you?"

"No. I helped them with their Lean transition, but they didn't report to me."

Fred leaned back and relaxed a little. "Was the transition to Lean different when you weren't in control of the other areas?"

"It sure was. It was much more difficult because of turf wars. I was spoiled in my first Lean transformation because of my control over accounting and manufacturing. But that company was different from Tricor."

"In what way?"

"It was much smaller."

"Oh. How about the other companies? What do you mean by turf wars?"

"I'm not going to sugarcoat it Fred. When I didn't have dual responsibility, the implementation process was a bitch. Accounting, finance, and IT had their own agendas and never had time for Lean. It made the journey very difficult. That's probably why I came down so hard on your group."

"I'm beginning to understand."

Mike continued, "I really enjoy the manufacturing challenge, but I hate having to convince the rest of the organization of the need to change. It's so difficult because everything's the opposite of what you've been taught."

"Didn't you ever have a problem changing?"

"That's an interesting question."

"Why?"

"In retrospect, I realize I readily embraced the new manufacturing methods, but when I sought out advice about accounting issues, I occasionally found myself going on the defensive because of my experience in that area."

"That's weird."

"No, it's not. I swear, sometimes I think that the more you know about a subject, the harder the Lean transition is. That's what makes it so difficult."

"I appreciate your sharing this with me. It would've been a lot easier if we had this discussion first."

"Hindsight is always twenty-twenty. If I could start over I would. I just got so excited about getting on with the process that I overlooked the most important thing, my teammates. We can't complete the journey unless we're a team, and I certainly didn't promote that aspect of Lean, did I?"

"You sure didn't. We'll get over it as long as it's the last time you act like a jerk."

Mike had a good laugh and some of the other Tricor employees noticed.

Fred continued, "My team will support the process if they see us supporting each other, not attacking one another as you did."

"OK, enough. I was wrong and I'm sorry. It won't happen again."

"Apology accepted, let's move on."

Fred and Mike reached over the table and shook hands. "That'll give everyone something to talk about, won't it?" asked Mike, grinning from ear to ear.

"I'm counting on it."

Their waitress, Connie, approached the table again.

"I thought you were never going to order! We have a business to run, you know." Connie served Fred for years and liked to joke with him. Fred introduced Mike and they engaged in some small talk. They took a few minutes to place their orders before continuing their conversation. Fred ordered his usual, while Mike ordered Wonton Soup and Triple Delight, a combination dish.

"What did you order?" asked Mike.

"The usual, Chicken and Lobster Sauce."

"I've never seen Chicken and Lobster Sauce on a Chinese menu."

"It's not on the menu. I'm probably the only one who has ever ordered it."

"I've heard of Shrimp and Lobster Sauce. Why the substitution?"

"I love Shrimp and Lobster Sauce, but I developed an allergy to shrimp a few years ago. Connie explained that there really isn't any lobster in Lobster Sauce, so they substitute chicken for the shrimp. It's really good."

"It sounds like they take care of you here."

"They do, and that's why I keep coming back."

"How long have you been eating here?"

"About twenty years now."

"Really," gasped Mike. "In all that time, has the restaurant ever been out of an item you ordered?"

"I never thought of that, but now that you mention it, I can't recall it ever happening."

"Have you ever had to wait long for your meal?"

"No."

"Has it ever arrived at your table cold?"

"Not really. So...."

"This restaurant's a good example of how a Lean operation functions."

"What?"

"Let me explain. From a limited number of ingredients they prepare a tremendous variety of dishes, or finished product. Each dish is cooked to order so it comes to the table piping hot, without the use of any finished goods inventory. The large variety of menu items can be cooked by any of the chefs, as they've all been cross-trained. And remarkably, the dishes taste the same regardless of the cook, because the process has been standardized..."

"What are you getting at?"

"Let me finish."

"Go ahead."

"The meals are prepared in only a few minutes because the set-up time for each dish is negligible. In fact, the same utensils and wok are rinsed in place and used again to eliminate set-ups. As a result, the customer gets a freshly cooked meal in minutes. Finally, since the menu remains fairly constant and the number of customers is fairly predictable, planning is relatively easy. The restaurant doesn't care what the customer orders, as long as they have sufficient raw material inventory. And since we're dealing with perishable foods, I bet if we hung around the restaurant all morning, we'd find that the raw materials are delivered each day, if not multiple times during the day."

"I never thought about it that way. Is that what you manufacturing guys think about all the time?"

"I hope not."

"I guess we just take it for granted. It's quite an efficient operation. That's probably why the prices are so reasonable."

"Bingo."

They paused as their soup was brought to the table. "This is my favorite part of the meal. I love Wonton Soup," said Mike. "Let me explain Lean at the highest level. Lean has five fundamental tenets, which include Value, the Value Stream, Flow, Pull, and Perfection."

"I vaguely recall that from the Lean class we had."

"Good. But the class was theory and everyone was getting bored."

"You noticed?"

"Sure I did. No one wants to listen to that stuff. Bear with me."

"Go ahead. I'll enjoy my soup."

"As I said, this restaurant's a good example of a company executing in a Lean fashion. They deliver value at an appropriate price or you wouldn't keep coming back for twenty years. They know their customers and provide terrific service as demonstrated by Connie. As for the value stream, they're very efficient in transforming raw material into a finished product. Everything appears to flow based on the pull of the customer with no finished goods warehouse. And I'm sure they continually try to improve, or as we say in Lean terms, strive for perfection. This is a good example of what we need to do at Tricor."

"How can you compare a Chinese restaurant to an electronics manufacturing company? Our business is so much more complex."

"Sure, it'll be harder to achieve at Tricor, but firms with more difficult challenges have implemented Lean, and so can we. Imagine how much more efficient we'd be if we could develop product that fast and then produce at the same rate the customer wants it, and for the lowest possible cost."

"You're dreaming, Mike.

"Sure I'm dreaming, but we can make it happen," said Mike as he leaned over the table, head jutted forward and eyes as big as silver dollars.

"Don't get so excited. You're making it seem too easy."

"I didn't say it would be easy."

"It'll take years, maybe decades. Who the hell has that kind of patience?"

"You're right. A transformation isn't done overnight, no matter how hard I push. It'll take at least five to ten years before we start approaching World Class results, and another decade or two of continuous improvements before we can even think about getting close to perfection."

"Maybe you're willing to devote decades to this, but I'm retiring soon. What can I realistically accomplish in three years?"

"If we work together, a great deal. Don't take this wrong, but I bet you'll see more improvements in the next three years than in the previous twenty years."

"Now don't go and start pissing me off again," cautioned Fred.

"Sorry about that. But please, spend some time with your staff discussing the questions I gave you. When you're ready to discuss them, let me know. I promise, it'll be a productive meeting."

"I'll give it a try," conceded Fred. "It'll take about a week. But I'm warning you, any funny business and I'll walk out of the meeting."

"It's a deal."

Mike and Fred finished their meal and spent time discussing their families. They had enough of Lean for one day.

Fred arrived home that evening and had a long talk with Sheila. He wasn't excited about spending the next three years working on a project that apparently goes on forever.

"Maybe it's time to retire now. We may not be able to afford everything we planned, but we'll still have a very comfortable retirement," said Fred.

"You've spent your entire life trying to be the best CFO possible, and now you're thinking of retiring because of Mike. Is it Mike or the challenge?"

"I think he's after my job. He told me he has a finance and accounting background, and the Lean transformation goes much smoother when he controls everything."

"Did you ask him about it?"

"Not directly. He knew I was concerned and said Tricor's too big for him to manage both areas."

"So why don't you believe him?"

"I don't trust him. He seemed sincere at lunch, and we had a good conversation, but he's so aggressive. You know how those manufacturing guys are— they brute-force everything."

"I'm sure he has enough to do to straighten out manufacturing. He doesn't need any more headaches. What's gotten into you? So you can retire now, what would you do? These could be the most exciting years of your career. Give him a chance and see what happens."

"If I don't see any real improvements, I'm going to talk to Peter about early retirement."

"It's your decision, but you have too much invested to leave over this. Mike must really be getting to you. Are the other department heads having the same problems with him?"

"Randy's a little concerned, but Mike hasn't been spending nearly the same amount of time in Product Development as he has in my area. Some of Mike's own people are worried as well, particularly the manufacturing engineers. They've heard they might lose their offices and they're upset."

"What do you mean?"

"Mike wants them to sit on the production floor so they're part of the floor teams."

"Well, at least it sounds like he isn't just picking on your area."

"That's for sure."

"Talk to your friends at the accounting firm and see if they can find some other companies that've gone through this program. See what they have to say."

"I've tried, but haven't had any success. I'll keep looking."

"Good. I'll support whatever you decide."

"Thanks, that means a lot."

9 World Class Road Trip

Mike was working on the computer when the phone rang. "What's up Fred?"

"I just found out Mary's in the hospital with pneumonia. She won't be able to go to Philly."

"Shit! How's she doing?"

"She's on antibiotics. She'll be out at least another week."

"That's too bad. I was looking forward to getting to know her better. Since we have a seat reserved, can you send someone else from accounting?"

"Can't she go another time? We're already short-handed."

"The next tour isn't for six months. Can't you spare someone for a day?"

"If it's that important, I'll send Scott Faulkner, the General Accounting Manager. He'll fill Mary in. But it better be worth it."

"Don't worry, it'll be a good experience for him."

The trip to Philadelphia was uneventful. The Lean champion of the facility, Tracy, escorted the tour group into the cafeteria and explained the company's Lean philosophy. On the walls were all sorts of charts and graphs, lists of projects with due dates and responsible parties, and an assortment of pictures and slogans. Tracy explained that Lean activities were posted in the cafeteria so the employees, or team members, could see what was going on. She was a bundle of energy, and it was apparent she played an instrumental role in the success of the facility.

Tracy led the tour group through the plant and had the shop-floor team members explain the improvement projects. The distinction between shop-floor personnel and management was blurry at best, as almost everyone in the plant was empowered to solve problems.

Upon entering the shop floor, everyone was awestruck at what seemed like a frenetic pace. It was difficult to find any muda in this plant. No one had ever witnessed such levels of activity.

Tracy explained that it only seemed frenetic because the typical manufacturing company manager was not accustomed to seeing a shop floor where the waste had been removed. Employees didn't wander around looking for tools or material, material handlers didn't load forklifts or use cranes, and no one walked around looking for a terminal to enter data. As the day progressed, the group became accustomed to the pace, and what initially seemed frenetic was beginning to seem normal.

Mike was concerned about Scott's reaction; he wasn't very familiar with Lean concepts.

"So, Scott, how's the tour going?" Mike asked as they lagged behind the rest of the group.

"Fine, but it's really different from our place. I don't see any shop-floor packets and I don't see anyone entering data into computers. How does accounting keep track of everything?"

Tracy waved them along so as not to hold up the rest of the group. "We'll have to ask about that later," said Mike, as they caught up to everyone.

The group moved to a section of the building where space had been freed up as a result of Lean activities. They took part in a game that simulated the transition from traditional manufacturing to Lean. As expected, the Lean group had better customer service, lower inventories, increased productivity, and of course, less space. What was accomplished in a few short hours in the simulation had taken place in this plant over the last ten years, and it was remarkable.

Later in the day, the group "toured" the administrative area, which consisted of an open bullpen with no offices, not even for Human Resources or the President. There weren't many people in this area because the role of management had changed over the years. Again, the group was shocked. Tracy explained that the engineers and product development folks had moved to the production floor, purchasing took place at the receiving dock, and production planning and inventory control were accomplished via a pull system on the production floor. The accounting portion of the bullpen consisted of only three people.

At the conclusion of the tour, the group reconvened in the cafeteria for a question and answer session. One person in the group asked, "Why's engineering located on the production floor?"

"Good question," responded Tracy. "The engineers have desks on the production floor because they support manufacturing. Since we have so little inventory, every product has to flow smoothly through all the operations. If there's a problem, the operator turns on an andon light..."

"What's an andon light?" asked someone from the group.

"It's a visual signal for help. If the engineers sat in the office, they'd never see the andon light, nor could they respond fast enough. It's more efficient for them to sit by the area they support so they're intimate with the products and are always 'on call'."

"Why aren't there any offices?" asked another

member of the tour.

"We don't need them," responded Tracy. "Just like on the production floor, communication is much easier when everyone's close together."

"What if you need to have a private conversation?" asked someone else.

"Then you use the conference room. Listen, I know you don't like to hear this, but it works much better. Give it a chance. Try it at your company."

There was a lot of chatter in the room. "Next question. You, in the back of the room."

"How has accounting changed?" asked Scott.

"The formal recordkeeping system has been simplified. The operators monitor the critical information, or performance metrics, at the work cells. The information's updated hourly so anyone walking through the plant knows how the area's performing."

Scott pressed on and Mike nodded in approval. "Do you have a perpetual inventory system?"

"No, it's not necessary. Our inventory turns so fast there's no need to track it. There's never much here anyway."

"So how do you know when to order material?"

"You are persistent, aren't you? As I showed you in the plant, we have kanban cards for every item. The water spiders deliver the cards to the folks by the receiving dock and they fax the information to our vendors."

"Do you have a formal cost system?"

"That's your last question," said Tracy somewhat seriously. Scott shrugged off the comment.

"We don't have a formal cost system. We use sample data to determine product costs. It's easier and a lot cheaper. Our costs are continuously declining anyway, so any standard cost would be wrong. We're interested in product family profitability rather than in individual item costs and we don't waste time tracking all the details."

Mike scanned the audience. The question and answer session on accounting left puzzled looks on the faces of most members of the tour group. He knew no one accepted Tracy's answers. They were too simple.

On the bus ride home, Mike turned toward Scott, who was looking out the window.

"So, Scott, what did you think?"

"It was interesting, but I don't understand what they're doing."

"Like what?"

"How can you operate without a perpetual inventory? It doesn't make sense."

"It does for them. They have so little inventory that they can count it in three hours. And since it moves through the plant so fast, why track it?"

"I heard what Tracy said, but I'm still not sure I understand their ordering rules."

"It's simple; they replace whatever they use. And since they produce to customer order, they can never order too much."

"But if the vendor doesn't deliver in time, won't it all come to a screeching halt?"

"Great question. They've spent the last ten years reducing their vendor base by seventy-five percent. The remaining vendors are reliable and have developed their own Lean processes. Between the company and the vendor there are about two to three week's worth of inventory in the pipeline, enough to cover most any problem. Does that make it any clearer?"

"It helps, but I still don't understand the mechanics of it all."

"It's very difficult to understand how it works when you see it for the first time. Don't worry, we'll implement the changes gradually over the next few years. We'll learn as we go."

Chapter 9

"Sounds like quite a challenge."
"It sure the hell is. But the rewards are awesome."

Mike thought about the trip the rest of the way home. He knew he'd have to do a lot of hand-holding with the accounting folks. He wondered if he had the patience to do this again.

10 World Class Fiasco

A few days later, Fred called Mary to see how she was doing.

"Hello," whispered Mary from her hospital bed.

"Hi, Mary," responded Fred. "I can hardly hear you. Should I call back later?"

"No, it's OK. I was just dozing," said Mary as she adjusted her pillow, took a sip of water, and sat up to speak.

"How you doing?"

"I'm still weak and sore all over, but I feel a lot better than I did a few days ago."

"That's good. Scott and the rest of the department have pitched in to cover your area."

"Yeah, I know. Scott called a couple of times to ask some questions."

"I hope he's not bothering you too much."

"It's not a problem."

"Good. By the way, did he mention the trip to Philly?"

"He sure did."

"What's wrong?"

"He's got me worried."

"Why?"

"He thinks cost accounting won't be needed in a Lean company."

"What!" exclaimed Fred.

"That's what he said."

"That can't be right. I'll have a talk with him. In the meantime, don't worry about it. Just concentrate on getting better."

"It's hard to ignore what he said."

"Please, don't worry about it. You have enough to worry about..."

"I have to go, the nurse is here to take some readings...."

"Take care."

Mike was in his office reviewing some reports when the telephone rang. He grabbed the receiver and listened to Fred, who was close to panic.

"Mike, what the hell went on during the trip to Philly? My department's up in arms again."

"Slow down. What are you talking about?"

"I just spoke with Mary at the hospital..."

"How's she doing?" interrupted Mike, wondering what this had to do with the trip.

"She's fine, damn it. That's not what I called about. She spoke with Scott and he told her cost accounting wouldn't be needed with Lean."

"What? You've gotta be kidding."

"Not at all. What are you trying to do? I have a key employee recuperating in a hospital and now she's worried that her job will be eliminated because of Lean."

"Slow down Fred. Nobody said that. And besides, why would I offer to take Mary if that was the intended message? Do you think I'm a fool?" Mike's brain was racing now. He thought he had patched everything up with Fred, but now this.

"Well then, what happened?"

"Scott was confused. The role of the cost accountant will definitely change, and for the better, but believe me, we'll still need Mary. Give me her telephone number and I'll talk to her."

Fred let out a big laugh, "Do you think I'm crazy? For someone who's been through this three times, you sure know how to screw it up. You really had me convinced at lunch a couple of weeks ago. I thought you knew what you were doing."

"Please, let me talk to her before she spends too much time worrying about it. I can't make the situation any worse."

"I'm not so sure about that."

"C'mon, gimme a break."

"I hope I don't regret this. Here's her number. Don't screw it up."

"Thanks." He hung up the telephone and was already thinking about what he'd say to Mary. He was trying to improve his relationship with accounting and it had taken another step backwards. He had to call Mary right away and straighten things out.

"Hello."

"Hi, is that you Mary?"

"Yes, who's this?"

"It's Mike Rogers. I was calling to see how you're doing."

"I'm feeling a little better."

"Great. Did you hear about the trip?"

"Yeah, Scott told me about it. He said you wouldn't need a cost accountant once Lean was implemented. Is that really why you're calling?"

Mike was glad Mary got right to the point. "Yeah, I don't want you worrying about anything. Scott's right, the job will gradually change, but I guarantee it'll be for the better."

"You're not just saying that, are you?"

"I wouldn't lie to you. You'll have more fun and do more challenging work. You'll be involved with the folks on the floor and participate in improvement efforts that make a real difference. If you like manufacturing, Lean will stretch you to the limit. And from what I've heard about you, you're up to the challenge."

"That's great, but it's not what Scott said."

"I know. It's tough to absorb everything during one trip. Just because Scott didn't see a bunch of people sitting in accounting doesn't mean they were all fired. They're still there, but doing things on the production floor like everyone else."

"Like what?"

"They're leading improvement teams, running kaizens, and closing the books. They're also analyzing acquisition candidates, which becomes part of the Lean strategy as cash, space, and capacity is freed up. Besides, it'll take years to get to that point anyway."

"That's a lot different from what Scott said. I want to do something else besides cost accounting anyway."

"Lean will be a real eye-opener, trust me."

"Since I'll be laid up for another week, do you have any Lean books I can read? It'll help pass the time."

"I'll see what I can find and get them over to you. Hope you're back soon."

After talking with Mary, Mike couldn't wait to call Fred.

"Fred, I just spoke to Mary and everything will be fine."

"I hope you're right. She's a smart lady, so don't try to pull anything over on her; it'll backfire."

"I'd never do that. If anything, I'm too direct. You should realize that by now."

"Maybe direct's not the right word. Never mind. I'll touch base with Mary and get back to you if there's a problem. What did you tell her?"

"The truth, that we need her."

"Honest?" needled Fred.

"You have my word."

11 Nocturne

The accounting department meeting was delayed until Mary returned, so Mike turned his attention to dealing with Tricor's suppliers. Tricor purchased a large number of component parts at fairly steady rates and Mike knew he could drastically simplify the process by employing the methods used at his prior company. He headed to Jim's office to discuss his plan.

"Jim, do you have a few minutes?" asked Mike.

Jim looked up from his desk, "Sure, boss, what's up?"

"Have you been tracking our shortages?"

"Are you kidding?" responded Jim as he reached for a marked-up computer report and handed it to Mike. "Look at this crap. No matter how hard we try, we're always out of parts. Purchasing busts their butts, but it's the same old story—give me the parts and I'll make the product. It never happens here."

Mike glanced at the report and sat down in the guest chair across from Jim.

"Make yourself comfortable, boss. I guess we're gonna have a nice little chat now."

"Why do you think we're always out of parts?"

"Listen, you know how overworked everyone is. We have thousands of parts, and the schedule's constantly changing, so there's no freakin' way the buyer/planners can keep up with everything. Something always falls through the cracks."

"We need to substitute smart work for hard work."

"Don't give me that business school crap."

Mike laughed. He was getting used to Jim and was glad he didn't mince his words. "If I can show you how to reduce shortages, and at the same time ease your workload, would you try it?"

"Sure, I'd be crazy not to, but it sounds too easy. What's the catch?"

"No catch. It's simple and it's easy once everyone's used to it. We'll try out my idea with some high volume parts purchased from a couple of vendors."

"What do I have to do?"

"Organize a meeting for tomorrow and I'll explain the process and show a demo. We'll need the buyer/planners and, since they report to you we shouldn't have any turf issues."

"Anyone else?"

"Debbie, Christy, and whoever pays the bills in accounting. Also, do me a favor and convince Fred to attend."

"Why do you want me to ask him?"

"I'm on thin ice with him."

"I thought you patched things up with him, boss."

"I did too, but my trip with Scott backfired. I need your help."

"I'll do my best. How about nine in the conference room tomorrow morning?"

"Works for me. See you then."

As Mike left Jim's office, he made a mental list of what he had to do to implement a trial "pull" system for purchased parts. At Mike's last company, he utilized the Internet for the process and it worked wonders. Mike was aware of the problems that would be encountered, as his first attempt was full of issues that were resolved on the fly. He wanted a problem free-implementation this time.

The next morning, everyone including Fred, gathered in the conference room. Mike made a mental note to ask Jim how he convinced Fred to attend.

Christy set up a laptop computer with a projector and Internet connection, as Mike had requested.

Mike opened the meeting. "Thanks for coming. I want to explain the use of kanbans to replenish material."

"What's a kanban?" asked one of the planner/buyers who had missed the intro class.

"Kanbans are visual signals that notify the upstream supplier that the customer needs more parts. Kanbans take many forms, but the easiest way to visualize them is to think of one process returning an empty container to the preceding process to be refilled. The upstream process never produces anything until the downstream process, or customer, signals the requirement via the empty container. Then they produce product to fill the empty container, and not one unit extra."

"That sounds pretty simple, but there must be a lot more to it," said Jim.

"It is simple. That's the way milk used to be ordered when the deliveryman made his rounds to each home, or so I've been told."

"That was before our time," quipped Christy, and everyone laughed.

"It was before my time also," said Mike. "But it worked. The customers simply put out as many empty bottles as they wanted to replace and the milkman left the same number of full bottles at the front door. The empty bottles were the kanbans."

"We're not selling milk. It's a lot more complicated here," said Debbie shaking her head.

Mike responded, "Sure it is, but if we follow some simple rules, we won't have any problems. We'll start with our external suppliers."

"I think I understand how the kanbans work," said Fred, "but how are we invoiced, how do we keep track of everything, what happens to the MRP-generated requirements? It sounds like a huge challenge."

"It sure does," agreed Debbie.

"You're right, Fred. Many of the changes can be implemented faster on the production floor than in the office."

"Ain't that the truth," said Jim as he stood up and paced at the back of the room.

Mike continued, "When I first attempted this, we ran into all sorts of accounting problems."

"Like what?" asked Scott.

"Our suppliers were ready to cut us off because we couldn't meet our payment commitments."

Christy chimed in next. "Mike, are you saying we just ignore the MRP requirements? Doesn't it get very confusing for the planner/buyers? Also, how does the supplier know how much to send us, when to send it, and when the requirements, or kanban quantities, need to be changed? The suppliers don't make a milk run to our plant every day, they ship the product via commercial carriers."

"One question at a time Christy. It'd be much easier if our suppliers were located a couple of hours from our plants, but I know that's not the case."

"I wish they were," exclaimed Debbie. "But we have suppliers all over the world."

"I know. It won't work for everyone," conceded Mike. "But it'll work for a lot of them, regardless of location. When the kanban's empty at the plant, we'll fax the supplier to trigger a delivery. A lot of companies use a simple fax system. But I'm proposing a much easier method utilizing the Internet. Let me show you what I mean and you'll understand it a lot better."

Mike turned on the computer and projector and

dialed up an Internet site. "The Internet's really simplified the use of kanbans with external suppliers. Here's the software we used at my last company. It radically changed they way we signaled our suppliers to replenish inventory. We used an ASP model so there are hardly any start up issues."

"It's never that easy, Mike," warned Christy.

"This routine is." Christy shook her head in disagreement, but Mike ignored her.

"What does ASP mean?" asked one of the planner/buyers.

"ASP is Application Service Provider. It means we'll be renting software that resides on someone else's computer," responded Christy.

"Thanks, Christy," said Mike. "We used, I mean rented, a software package called Nocturne which resided at a host site. Each night our inventory data was automatically downloaded to the Nocturne software and was available to our suppliers. They saw our consumption, and based on pre-set rules, decided when to ship us more parts. There were no purchase orders, no telephone calls, no confirmations, and no MRP messages to deal with."

"What kind of rules?" asked Debbie.

"Let me show you." Mike opened a demo site and projected a page onto the screen. He grabbed the laser pointer and continued. "For each supplier, each part's listed with the minimum and maximum inventory levels. Next to each part is what looks like a gas gauge that indicates the part status."

"How does that work?" asked Jim.

"It's simple."

"Everything's simple according to you," insisted Fred in a mocking way.

Mike ignored the comment. He thought it best to eat some crow until he won Fred over again. He went on with his explanation, and everyone relaxed.

"If the gauge is red, the supplier knows he has to deliver parts ASAP because the inventory has dropped below the minimum quantity. If the gauge is yellow, the inventory is less than halfway between the lower and upper limit, and the supplier can deliver immediately or wait a little longer. And if the gauge is green, the inventory level's fine and the supplier doesn't have to do anything. The supplier has visibility to what's happening at the plant every day. We don't have to do a thing."

"I like it," said Debbie, "but what about the purchase orders?"

"Mike, what about spikes in demand? How can the supplier keep up?" asked Jim.

"What if we redesign the part?" asked Fred.

The questions kept coming.

"Good questions, but the answers aren't any different in an MRP environment."

"What do you mean?" asked Debbie.

Mike was about to say "it's simple" but he caught himself in time. "This method means the supplier replenishes inventory as the customer consumes the product, or "pulls" it from our finished goods. If you change the part, you'll have to notify the supplier, just like with an MRP system. And I guarantee there will be fewer parts in the pipeline with this system than if ordering from a forecast via MRP.

"I think I understand, but what about my question about spikes in demand?" said Jim impatiently.

"With spikes in demand, you'll be in better shape with this system. If the spike is a total surprise, then the information will be communicated instantaneously as the supplier sees consumption increasing. It's a lot quicker than waiting for an official MRP update, which can take a week or two."

"If we're lucky," yelled out Jim.

Mike ignored the comment and continued with his

explanation. "If the spikes can be forecast, then you can post a note right next to the part number to notify the supplier and he'll acknowledge it per your instructions. As for purchase orders, you prepare a blanket order at the beginning of the year and all deliveries are against the blanket. A lot of paperwork, or muda, is eliminated."

"What are the trouble spots?" asked Fred.

Fred's question brought a smile to Mike's face. I've got his attention now, he thought.

"When we first implemented this, everything worked well except the accounting routines. As part of our program we told the suppliers we'd pay in ten days if we received an early pay discount. We viewed this as an opportune time to negotiate better terms."

"What did that have to do with Lean?" asked Scott.

"Nothing and everything," responded Mike. "Early pay discounts have nothing to do with Lean, but the implementation pointed out some shortcomings in accounting. We wanted better terms in exchange for paying early and eliminating a lot of supplier paperwork. Most of the suppliers agreed to the discount and delivered parts per the pre-established rules. After about forty-five days, we started getting complaints that we weren't paying on time. Our suppliers threatened to eliminate the early pay discount."

"Why didn't you adhere to your end of the bargain?" asked Fred.

"Accounts Payable processed checks on the fifteenth and thirtieth of the month, and if cash was tight, they held off mailing the checks for a few days. Since accounting was operating in a batch mode, they couldn't meet the quick pay guidelines."

"I guess you didn't check with accounting first," said Fred.

"Guilty as charged," acknowledged Mike. "After calming down the suppliers we made the necessary changes and paid everyone in exactly ten days."

"What changes did you make?" asked Debbie.

"We treated the accounts payable process like a manufacturing operation and made sure the work flowed based on the pull of the customer. In this case, the customers for the output of accounts payable were the suppliers, and the signal that triggered the work was the material receipt. Accounts payable could no longer operate in a batch mode and accumulate bills for up to fifteen days before processing them. If necessary we'd process checks daily. So you see, accounting has the same challenges as manufacturing in trying to achieve flow, which is the ability to process one part, or in this case, one transaction at a time, economically, based upon the pull of the customer."

Fred responded, "But it's more efficient to batch all the payments."

"Not really," said Mike. "That's the kind of thought process we have to reverse. It's no different than what's done in the plant every day. I've spent years preaching the same thing to everyone who operates large pieces of equipment."

"Now what do you mean?" asked Jim. "You're jumping from accounting to equipment."

"Bear with me. Everyone in the machine shop and production planning has been taught to process large batches to amortize set-up costs over long runs, whether we have customer orders or not. Isn't that true, Jim?"

"Yeah, so what?"

"Nobody's attacking the root cause of long runs, which is long set-up times. Lean manufacturing has a number of tools and techniques that attack set-up reduction, so multi-hour set-ups can be reduced to ten minutes or less. With this paradigm shift, the need for long production runs and large equipment disappears, and the entire planning process has to be re-evaluated. That's exactly what we did in the Accounts Payable department. We changed the process so we could process checks daily. Lean concepts apply everywhere."

Mike scanned the room. At least everyone appeared to be paying attention.

Fred continued probing, "I hope you had the funds to absorb the one-time cash outflow for the quick pay program. We don't have the cash flow to do it."

"Manufacturing took some heat from accounting, but not for long."

"Why, what happened?" asked Debbie.

"Within three months, we lowered our inventory enough to compensate for the initial cash outflow," responded Mike rather proudly as he looked at Fred.

Fred reluctantly nodded in approval, as did the others in the room. "Don't do anything without running it by me first or we're likely to get in trouble with our banks." warned Fred.

"I won't," agreed Mike.

Mike could tell Scott was still uncomfortable. "Scott, is this starting to make sense now?"

"It's a little clearer. How did you start the inventory reduction program?"

"With the help of our software vendor, we started out with what I'll call the 150/150 test plan. We took 150 part numbers and monitored the inventory levels for 150 days. The results were astonishing. Within the first 150 days, the inventory of test parts was cut in half, which, from a cash flow perspective, dwarfed the impact of the early pay program. And, the prepayment discounts provided a terrific return on the initial cash outflow."

"Of course they do," said Fred, "but sometimes we're not in a position to accelerate payments due to borrowing limitations."

"I understand. That's why I explained that the cash drain is only a short-term issue. We'll benefit twice—first from the early pay discount and second from the reduced inventory investment. You can bank on it!"

"You're scaring me again, Mike. Whenever this Lean stuff starts to sound too good, I get suspicious," said Fred. The rest of the room laughed.

Mike was excited and forgot that this was a demo meeting, not an implementation planning session. "Fred, let's start with a small sample of items and monitor the situation. That's also part of the Lean culture. We call it PDCA, or Plan it, Do it, Check the results against baseline measures, and then Act accordingly to continually improve the process. Lean's action-oriented."

Fred shifted uncomfortably in his chair. "You're getting ahead of yourself, Mike. We're still trying to absorb all of this."

"You're right. I'll answer all your questions first."

"That would help," replied Fred.

"OK then, let's move on. Lowering the inventory led to two more problems."

"What were they?" asked Christy.

"As I said, our inventories were cut in half five months after implementing the program. What was good news for us was terrible news for our suppliers."

"I don't understand," said Scott.

"We convinced our suppliers to embrace this new program in the interests of their business, and then the order flow from our company was cut in half. They really didn't understand the program and thought we were in serious trouble, when in fact, everything was working fine. We should've warned them to expect the inventory reduction. It was a big mistake."

"I can imagine the phone ringing off the hook in Purchasing," said Debbie. What was the other problem?"

"Lowering inventory always exposes problems. You discover parts that haven't moved in a while and are obsolete. I don't care how good your records are; I've yet to work at a company that didn't have an inventory write-down as a result of lowering inventory, and it's impossible to predict the magnitude of the problem, so you keep your fingers crossed."

"Is that a technical term?" joked Fred.

"Just the truth."

"That doesn't make me feel any better. We can't embark on such a program without knowing the financial ramifications. We're under such pressure to meet earnings projections, I can't surprise everyone with an inventory write-down."

"I agree," said Mike. He knew from first-hand experience that surprises were taboo in the financial area. "That's something we'll have to work on. If we go ahead with a small group of parts, maybe we can find out the extent of the problem. The slower a company's inventory turns, the greater the risk for inventory obsolescence. And I'm afraid Tricor's risk is fairly high."

"Anything else?" asked Debbie.

"Sure, change is never easy. When we fixed the accounts payable process we had to catch up on a lot of payments. As we made the payments based on our parts receipt information, our suppliers called in a panic. They couldn't figure out how to apply the payments."

"Why?" interrupted Scott.

"They were used to receiving payments that referenced an invoice number and we paid based upon packing slips. Needless to say, our supplier's collection folks were confused."

"So what did you do?" asked Christy.

"We asked the suppliers to number their packing slips so we could reference them on the check stubs. Then they could accurately apply the payments. In retrospect, it was fortunate we implemented the early pay program; it brought the problem to light much sooner than if we paid per our normal terms."

Tom Hilton, the Controller, had joined the group midway through the meeting. "If you're paying based upon packing slips, what happens to the invoices?"

"We told our suppliers to stop sending invoices,

they're muda. Pricing was per the blanket order and the payment was based on the receipt quantity. There was no need for an invoice."

"Wow, that's simple enough," said Debbie grinning from ear to ear. "No more triple matching problems. I love it!"

"It doesn't stop there. Next we established an electronic payment process based upon material receipts. And the ultimate goal is automatic payment to suppliers as you ship product to your customers based upon backflushing the bills of material. The product moves so fast, there's no need to track receipts."

"Now that seems a little far-fetched," said Tom. "Is anyone doing that?"

"Not that I know of," admitted Mike. "But I've heard some companies talking about it."

"There are always additional improvements to make," said Christy.

"Bingo! The pursuit of perfection, or the elimination of waste, is a never-ending challenge that stretches our ability to view things differently. That's what makes Lean so much fun!"

"I think I understand the accounting issues, but what about the rules for setting up kanbans?" said Jim.

"That's easy. We'll start with items that have fairly steady demand, build in an initial safety factor, and then slowly remove kanbans as we get comfortable with it. The initial kanban size will depend on supplier lead-times and usage rates."

"But what about the computer system?" continued Jim.

"We'll need Christy's help to tag the items managed via kanbans. Per past experience, the planners will get frustrated initially because they have to do double duty managing some parts via MRP and others via kanbans. But once they see how easy kanbans are, they'll want to convert all the parts to the new method as quickly as possible."

"I think I understand. What do you think?" said Jim looking toward the planners.

"We won't know until we try it," said one of the planners. But I can't imagine not using MRP. It'll be chaos."

"No, it won't. I'll help you with it," replied Mike.

The room went silent. Mike wondered if they were out of questions or totally overwhelmed. He never intended to cover so much material. He gave them one last chance. "Any other questions?"

"Just one. How did the suppliers like the system?" asked Fred.

"Once they got used to it, they loved it. They were better equipped to schedule their plants because they had much more data than before, and it was readily available. All shipment and usage data were available online and could be downloaded to Excel spreadsheets for analysis. Also, when we changed a product, there were hardly any parts in the pipeline, so inventory write-offs were negligible for both parties. It was a win/win situation, but it took time for the suppliers to realize it."

"How can we improve the launch?" asked Debbie.

Great, Debbie's already thinking about how she'll convince the suppliers, thought Mike.

"Good question. We'll hold supplier meetings before we implement anything. We didn't know enough to do that at my last company, nor did we have all the answers."

Mike glanced at his watch and realized they had been discussing Nocturne for two hours. "Let's wrap up. Using an Internet software solution is only one way to achieve these results. The company we visited in Philadelphia used faxes to achieve the same results. We have to pick the solution that's best for us, and from what I've seen so far, the Internet may be the way to go." Mike gathered his papers and shut down the computer. Everyone except Fred exited the conference room.

"Mike, it looks good, and I really like the financial benefits, but I'm concerned. You always seem to miss something."

"It'll go a lot smoother than at my last company. Plus we'll be testing it with about 150 parts. The nature of Lean is not to plan ad infinitum."

"I'm not comfortable with that. It's too risky."

"I promise, we'll take it one step at a time."

"I guess I'll have to cross my fingers," teased Fred. Mike had a good laugh and they both left the room.

Fred headed back to his office and met up with Tom and Christy.

"Sorry I couldn't get there earlier," said Tom.

"What did you think?"asked Fred.

"Mike has some good ideas. If Nocturne works it'll really help us."

"The jury's still out on that. How about you Christy?" askedFred.

"Hey, I loved it. It's state-of-the-art IT stuff. What more can I ask for? It just won't be as easy as he thinks."

"It never is," responded Fred. "Now I know why he needs our support. Without accounting and IT, electronic kanbans wouldn't be possible."

12 The Road Trip

Peter stopped by Fred's office to see how things were going. Peter was leaving on a three-week tour of Tricor's customers and was meeting with the Board and the stock analysts while in Boston and New York. He wanted to firm up the financial forecast prior to his departure. Peter had an understanding with Fred; Peter signed off on the sales forecast, and Fred forecasted the remainder of the P&L. Fred did it for twenty years and was extremely accurate. Peter had the tough part, the sales forecast.

"Do you have a few minutes, Fred?"

"Sure, what's up?"

Peter set his coffee mug on the corner of Fred's desk and pulled over a chair. "How are you and Mike getting along?"

"I finally had a productive meeting with him."

"Great! What was it about?"

"Setting up kanbans with our suppliers."

"Joe's a big fan of kanbans. I spoke to him the other day and he asked if we had set any up. He said they'll really improve cash flow."

"That's what Mike said. I hope they're right."

"They're the ones with the experience. Joe's gonna be looking for progress reports, so give Mike your full support."

"We're trying, but it's difficult with all the budget

work."

"Do the best you can. If you need to hire some temps, go ahead. I really want to get the kanbans going. I also want to talk to you about my meeting with some of the Board members next week. I need to give them a heads-up on next year's earnings outlook."

"I know. I'm wrapping that up now. You'll have it before you leave. When are you meeting with those jerks on Wall Street?" asked Fred sarcastically. He was referring to the two stock analysts who followed Tricor. At one time they were interested in understanding the business, traveled to corporate headquarters to review plans, crunched their own numbers, and provided insight. Nowadays they simply wanted Peter and Fred to hand-feed them the forecasts. They called it guidance. Fred longed for the good old days.

"Careful now. We have to stay on their good side. They can make or break us." It was the only area where Peter found fault with Fred's performance.

"I know, it's not their fault. We're just a small cap stock and they don't have time for us. Or as one of my friends used to say, the earth could open up and swallow the company and it wouldn't even make the back page of the *Wall Street Journal*."

"I wouldn't go that far. I'm meeting with them at the end of the week. How does it look?"

"I wish I had better news. The forecast hasn't improved from the preliminary numbers I gave you. At best we're looking at eight percent earnings per share (EPS) growth. Don't promise anything above six percent. We need a cushion with this lousy economy."

"I agree, but they're not gonna like it."

"As long as they aren't expecting anything more, go with six percent."

"They're always expecting more. The Board's a different story. We need eight percent growth to hit our internal target or Joe will start campaigning for my resignation."

"Boy, he can be a real pain in the ass!"

"It's not just him you know. From what I hear, he's picking up support. I'll tell the analysts six percent, but we better make it or our stock we'll take a beating. Are you sure it's safe to go with six percent?"

Fred raised his arms and shrugged. "C'mon, you know me, I'm never comfortable. There are only so many things I can do to add a penny or two to earnings, and, quite frankly, the cupboard is bare."

"You say that every year."

"Well, this time it's true. We don't have the good fortune of working with a one-year backlog. If we don't hit the sales forecast, we won't make the numbers. I'm out of financial tricks."

"Then we have to hit our sales numbers. Given our trends and new products, we'll be fine."

"You're always the optimist—how do you do it?" "When you come up through sales and marketing, you need to be an optimist, otherwise you won't survive. I've never met a good salesman that was a pessimist; the job would be impossible."

"I guess that's why I'm in accounting."

Peter smiled and nodded in agreement. "Let me know immediately if the forecast changes. We need to keep the Board informed, otherwise our credibility will tank."

"Come on; I know what you're up against. I've been raked over the coals plenty of times when we haven't met the numbers. If anything comes up, you'll be the first to know."

"Thanks."

"Thank you."

"For what?"

"For meeting with the analysts this time"

"I'd rather you wrap up the budget for the Board."

13 The Prep Session

"Let's get this over with," said Howard Lee, Manager of Budgeting and Financial Analysis. "I've got a ton of work to do to finish the budget."

"Christy and Tom are wrapping up a payroll issue. They'll be right down," said Fred.

"How long will this take?"

"Two hours at most. I want to make sure we're prepared for the meeting next week."

"Two hours!" said Howard shaking his head in disgust. "Do we really have to do this?"

"Yep. We're not going to BS Mike. He has a financial background and has been through all of this before."

"No kidding," said Scott. "No wonder he's all over the accounting reports."

"Damn right. Mary, have you had enough time to research Mike's questions?"

"I finished most of them before I got sick. I'm ready."

"Good."

"It's about time you two showed up," said Howard as Tom and Christy entered the conference room.

"What's with him?" said Tom.

"He's always cranky around budget time. Just ignore him," said Scott.

"We always do," responded Tom as he made his way around the table and sat next to his buddy Howard.

"Let's get going already," said Fred. "Let's go through the questions one by one. Who wants to go first?"

Mary volunteered. "It was easy to get the information about cost of sales," said Mary as she handed out some charts and graphs. "Our costs are fifteen percent direct labor, twenty percent overhead, and sixty-five percent material. I graphed the direct labor and overhead expenses for the past twenty-four months, as Mike suggested."

"I see that," said Howard, as he shuffled through the handouts.

Mary continued, "Monthly spending was flat, even when our volumes fluctuated, like they always do in the slower summer months."

"What do you make of that?" asked Howard.

"Mike probably wanted to prove that direct labor and overhead costs are relatively fixed within certain volume levels. I'm just not sure why."

Fred responded, "Let's go through the other items before we try to figure it out. What else Mary?"

"I thought about his question on costing accuracy. We spend a lot of time correcting bills of material, but there are always issues with purchase price variances, scrap reporting, and expensed items. Also, there are timing issues with material, as excess parts issued to the production floor are never returned to the stockroom in a timely manner, so it's hard to identify which product line should get the credit. It all adds up to some level of inaccuracy, but I don't know how much."

"How about direct labor?" asked Tom.

"The labor tracking system works well in assembly, but it depends entirely on the employees' clocking in and out of departments correctly. And there's always some gamesmanship going on because supervisors borrow people but don't get cross-charged for the labor as it's only a few hours here and there. Also, since labor's tracked by department, not by product or SKU, (stock keeping unit), it's only accurate at the product family level. It's not perfect, but it's good."

"Sounds like it can be improved," said Tom. "How about the Machine Shop?"

"The Machine Shop's a problem. We track labor, but we can't get all the information without spending a fortune. I talked to the operators and they said they try to properly record their time but make mistakes or forget, and then try to catch up at the end of the day."

"Can I help with anything?" asked Christy.

"Let's review everything before we look for solutions," said Fred as he motioned for Mary to continue.

"Finally, the overhead items are allocated as best as we can. You really can't defend the allocations for some items, like taxes, insurance, purchasing, and supervisory salaries. Even depreciation's suspect because there are so many methods, who's to say which method best reflects actual product costs."

"So, what's your verdict? Are costs accurate?" asked Christy.

Mary took a deep breath and scanned the room before answering. "Mike will have no problem pointing out deficiencies in our cost system; that's the easy part. I just don't know how he can improve it."

Christy wasn't satisfied. "Mary, if you had to guess, how accurate are our cost standards?"

"I haven't had time to work on that."

"From what I hear, Mike measures everything, so you better be prepared with an estimate."

"Christy's right," said Fred. "See what you can work up for the meeting."

"Not a problem," said Mary. "One more thing. I talked with the guys in the plant and found out how much time they spend clocking on and off jobs to collect costs. It's a lot!"

"Really. How much is it?" asked Fred.

"We spend about ten minutes per day per person clocking labor in the plant. With 500 hourly people, that's 20,000 hours per year, or almost a half million dollars!"

"Wow!" blurted out Scott. "That's a lot of money."

"It sure is," responded Mary. "And it doesn't include the admin costs to monitor the data, reconcile differences to payroll records, and post-month end corrections for the inevitable errors. It's costly and time consuming, and we've assumed manufacturing uses the information to manage the shop."

"I never thought about the cost to collect all of that data," acknowledged Tom.

"What about the rest of Mike's cost questions?" asked Howard.

"Can't get enough of this analysis stuff now, can you?" teased Tom.

"Look at him, he's the only one taking notes," said Christy laughing.

"Shut up and let Mary answer my question."

"Ignore 'em Howard," said Mary. "Mike was interested in the departmental statements, particularly the proportion of controllable vs. uncontrollable expenses. I think I know what he was alluding to. I've heard the supervisors complain they get beat up for unfavorable variances, but they don't have control over the spending."

"You've lost me," remarked Christy.

"I don't believe it," said Tom, snapping his head to the left and looking at Christy in amazement. "You're always two steps ahead of us."

"You're right, I am most of the time..."

"We'll be here all day if you don't let Mary finish," said Fred. "Go ahead Mary."

"Let me give you an example. John Winters, the supervisor in the sheet metal shop, is responsible for about two and a half million dollars a year. About sixty percent of his spending is related to overhead items such as depreciation, insurance, taxes and production management. When the sheet metal shop has a slow month, John's department has a lot of unfavorable variances and he complains that he really can't do anything about them."

"He's right," agreed Tom.

"He sure is," said Mary. "John has no control over those items, yet he has to explain his variances each month. He has only one alternative to improve the numbers. He can produce more product, whether we need it or not, to absorb overhead and minimize the unfavorable variances. Experienced supervisors used to do that to protect their numbers when they saw our volume slipping. That only led to further problems a month or two later."

"Like big increases in inventory," explained Howard.

"That's crazy Mary. You're telling me our supervisors keep producing when they shouldn't?"

"Of course. It happens in most manufacturing plants that build to a forecast. Since bonuses are driven by productivity measures, the operators and supervisors have an incentive to keep building product until the company revises the forecast. The fact that inventories increase the whole time is not their concern. We've been fortunate and haven't had to worry about that problem recently because of steady sales growth, but sooner or later every company faces this problem. When we have our next slowdown, it'll happen again."

"It's happened in the past, but our managers recognize the situation before it gets out of hand. I don't think it'll happen again," said Fred.

Mary didn't respond, but realized there wasn't any way to avoid the problem given the current measurement system. In the event of a slowdown, curtailing purchasing and reducing production levels would be like stopping an ocean liner. Sure, the company would eventually ratchet down the activity, but the process would drag on while forecasts were updated, MRP runs were analyzed, and vendors were contacted. It was time to move on or this meeting would never end.

"The last item was the question about operating expenses. Twenty percent, or thirty-three million dollars of product cost is overhead, and operating expenses are one hundred and eleven million dollars. Mike must wonder why we go through the trouble and expense of allocating overhead to discrete products yet ignore operating expenses, which are more than three times as large. If that's where he's headed, I agree with him."

"I do too," said Fred. "I don't understand why we spend so much money on sales and marketing. I'm sure our products require different levels of support, but we never take the time to analyze it."

"How would we do it?" asked Scott.

Fred responded, "We've never agreed on a method. That's the problem."

Everyone started to come up with suggestions but Fred cut them off. "That's not the purpose of this meeting. Let's wait and see what Mike has to say about it. Are you finished Mary?"

"That's all I have."

"Good job! Let's move on to the philosophical questions. Howard, let's start with you. Since you're in charge of budgeting and forecasting, you should have a good idea of the value of our reports. What do you think?"

Howard was at Tricor for the past five years. He was extremely dedicated, arriving at work each morning at six o'clock to get a head start on the daily reports. He was particularly adept at spreadsheet analysis and created much of Tricor's reporting structure. The budget was Howard's "baby" and the greater the complexity, the more enjoyable the challenge.

"I had lunch the other day with Jim and some of his supervisors and asked about the reports. I thought they were going to choke on their food."

"What do you mean?" asked Tom.

"They hardly use the reports. The only reason they look at them is to get ready for the month-end meeting with Mary and me. If not for the meeting, they could care less about them."

"So what do they use?" Tom wanted to know.

"I'll tell you," said Christy. "Ever since we put in the new system, I've been getting a steady stream of report requests from manufacturing. I thought the new reports were meant to supplement the existing reports, but evidently they've been building their own little reporting system."

"That's what they told me," said Howard. "They only use the accounting reports to satisfy us."

"But don't the variance reports help them identify problems in the plant?" asked Tom.

"No way. They even challenged me to list all of the variances calculated by the new system and define each one. I couldn't do it."

"I couldn't either," added Scott.

"Me neither," said Christy.

Howard continued. "Then they gave me a break and asked about an easy variance, labor. They wanted to know what the labor variances meant each month. According to them, by the time they get the numbers at month end the problem could be long gone. Also, they complained because the labor variance reports don't tell them which product had a problem or why, and whether it was getting better or worse."

"So what do they use?" asked Christy.

"They have their own methods, although they agreed they weren't much better. They want information that helps them get to the root cause of the problem."

"Don't we all," said Fred. "Does anyone else have any comments?"

"Yeah, I do," said Tom. "There's still one item we haven't discussed. Mike asked about the detailed expense reporting for wages and benefits. Now I think I know why he's questioning it."

"Go ahead," encouraged Fred.

"Each item, like medical benefits, vacation, holiday, payroll taxes, and the 401K match, has its own account number and is charged in detail to the departments. It takes a lot of time, and now I wonder why we do it."

"I see where you're headed," said Mary. "The supervisors have no control over the benefits, so they probably don't look at them anyway."

"Exactly. I bet Mike will suggest we allocate benefits in a lump sum and eliminate a lot of work. Why don't we do it that way now?"

"It's not that bad the way we do it," said Fred. "All the routines are already set up. Have you seen it done differently at any of the other companies you've worked for?"

"No, I haven't."

"We've talked about a lot of problems with accounting reports," said Mary. "It'll only get worse after Mike gets his chance."

"You're right," said Fred. "Maybe Mike will have some good ideas, but we have to make sure we don't lose our historical benchmarks. We'll be OK for the meeting next week."

The meeting adjourned and Fred thought about the discussion. My own staff criticized some of the current reporting schemes. Why did it take the prodding of Mike to get us to question our work? Am I so comfortable with current procedures that I can't see the forest for the trees? What will Mike have to say? After all, he's been through this many times. Fred dreaded the upcoming meeting.

Fred couldn't help but wonder about Mike's motives again. Was Mike an overanxious manufacturing executive trying to achieve some quick successes, or did he have a private agenda to expand his role at Tricor? Was Sheila correct in her assessment or was he naïve?

14 Inventory Reduction

Tricor had about forty million dollars of inventory and achieved only four turns per annum vs. an industry average of almost six turns. Inventory levels for some items were out of control due to forecast errors.

Mike's relationship with Peter and Fred was fragile and he wanted to demonstrate the benefits of Lean with a significant early "win." An improvement in inventory turns would result in an immediate increase in cash flow and help convince everyone of the merits of Lean. Mike decided to pursue this initiative aggressively, especially since there was such a favorable reception to his presentation of the Nocturne software.

Implementing the electronic kanban system would, in addition to decreasing inventory, facilitate the role of the production planners, simplify purchasing, and reduce part shortages. This was the easiest area to achieve some quick benefits and the learning curve was minimal. As part of his plan to attack this opportunity, Mike had Debbie analyze the supplier base to identify potential candidates for Nocturne. Tricor had four hundred vendors of which eighty, or twenty percent, accounted for eighty-five percent of the dollar volume. Fortunately, two of the vendors in the top ten supplied fairly simple parts, had excellent on-time performance, and supplied components that did not require incoming inspection. These two vendors were excellent candidates for testing the Internet-based system. They accounted for about five percent of annual material purchases, or about five million dollars.

Mike spoke to the software vendor and developed a rough systems implementation plan with Christy. The hardware and software would be operational in two weeks. It was time to get Debbie and Mary on board.

Mike, Mary and Debbie gathered in the Purchasing conference room.

"What the heck happened to you?" asked Mary as she stared at Mike's left arm.

"I was in a 50K bike race this weekend and took a spill. It's not as bad as it looks."

"Yeah, I bet. It must've hurt like hell."

"I was lucky, I just got a few scrapes. It could've been a lot worse."

"Do you do everything full speed ahead?"

"Hey, it was just a bike race."

"I'll stick to the gym, it's a lot safer."

"Let's get going already. I want to begin implementing the electronic kanban system. Debbie's identified two suppliers to test the process. Mary, you'll need to analyze our historical usage patterns by item number to establish the initial kanban quantities.

"I don't know how to do that," exclaimed Mary.

"I know. I'm gonna help you. We'll calculate an initial inventory quantity based on supplier lead times and consumption rates and add a safety buffer until we're comfortable. Then we'll reduce inventory by removing kanbans from the system until we reach the minimum level necessary to operate..."

"But Mike, what about the requirements called out by the MRP system?"

"For the kanban items we'll ignore the MRP signals. Instead we'll rely on our suppliers to automatically replenish inventory at a rate equal to our consumption. The information will be available to them on a daily basis via the Internet. And fortunately, we have very accurate inventory records; otherwise I'd never do this so soon."

"Why do we have to keep removing kanbans?"

"To identify the limits of the system. That's the best way to expose the next problem area. But don't worry, we'll focus on adding new items to reap the initial gains before we worry about removing kanbans. I just wanted you to understand process. We'll be busy adding items to the system for quite awhile.

Debbie, you'll need to schedule a meeting with both vendors ASAP to get the ball rolling. You'll also need to get accounts payable (A/P) on board to plan for early payments. I want discount terms for early payment as part of the initial roll out."

"Aren't you asking a lot from our suppliers? What if they object?" challenged Debbie.

"Sure they'll object, especially if they're not doing something similar with their other customers. It's only natural. But they'll benefit as well since they'll have a long-term commitment from us, visibility to our consumption patterns, or should I say our customers' consumption patterns, and the first opportunity to be part of a preferred supplier or partner program. We can't go down the Lean path and have a lot of suppliers for the same commodities. By participating now, they'll assure themselves of a long-term commitment."

"But if we give them annual commitments, how's that different from buying the inventory like we do now?"

"I'm glad you asked, Debbie, because unless you fully believe in the program, you won't be able to sell it to the suppliers."

"I'm trying, but I just don't know enough about it."

"Since the suppliers will see our consumption pattern, they won't be caught by surprise. For example, in an MRP environment, we order based on forecast and, if we overestimate, eventually orders come to a screeching halt. Our suppliers get stuck with work in process and raw material because they typically build safety stocks to accommodate our erratic order patterns. Then we all spend countless hours on the telephone negotiating new delivery dates. Does that sound familiar?"

"Yeah, that's what typically happens."

"With this system, that won't happen. Individual purchase orders and invoices will be eliminated, and the suppliers will require less overhead to manage the activity. As for annual commitments, we'll give the suppliers a range of commitments over a time period, say twelve to fifteen months, rather than ordering discrete quantities as we do now. Since we'll have less inventory and the supplier will have less inventory, the risk for both parties is reduced."

"Makes sense," said Debbie.

"I'd like both of you to work through the details with Christy, the software vendor, and the supplier. I want to be up and running in thirty days."

"What's the rush?" asked Mary.

"I'd like to get going so we can begin the new fiscal year with a head start. I'll work with Jim and the production planners to insure that everyone's on board." Mike glanced at his watch. "I've gotta run to another meeting. Call me if you have any other questions."

"So what do you think?" asked Mary.

"I'm scared as hell!" responded Debbie. "I've worked so hard to establish good relations with our suppliers. I hope this doesn't screw everything up."

"He must know what he's doing."

"We'll see."

Later that day Mike was sitting at his desk staring at his "to do" list on his whiteboard. He was getting a lot of the Lean techniques started but was behind in training. He knew he better not start any other initiatives until more people went through some basic Lean training, including a Lean overview and 5S procedures.

Mike also wondered why it always took so long for companies to implement kanbans. The process was so elementary that most companies couldn't believe the benefits, and dismissed the idea. He had always achieved tremendous gains, and so made it a practice to push kanbans at the beginning of his Lean implementations.

15 Overhead, Overhead

The last meeting with accounting was a disaster and Mike wanted to get his points across this time without offending anyone, especially Fred. Mike knew that manufacturing could implement Lean and achieve some isolated gains, but the journey would stall if the administrative areas were not fully committed to Lean as well. Mike needed their support and was determined to make the meeting a success.

Everyone who had attended the last meeting gathered in the Board Room to review Mike's questions. Joining Fred were Mary, Christy, Scott, Tom, and Howard. Accompanying Mike were Jim, Tim, Charles, and Debbie. There was no chit-chat and needling of each other as they walked into the room and took their seats.

Mike began. "I know you've been thinking about the questions from the last meeting. Rather than jump right into the detail, I'd like to start with an overview and then drill down into the specifics."

"What do you mean?" asked Fred, fidgeting in his seat.

"It'd be helpful if first we discussed the choice of a cost system—full absorption vs. material only costing. Is that OK?"

"It's OK with me," said Tom. "You're the one who wants to change everything. I'm curious to see what you have to say."

"We don't have time to go through basic account-ing theory," said Fred. "It's the busiest time of the year. We barely have enough time to finish the budget."

"Bear with me," insisted Mike. "It's important for us to understand the alternatives so we can make the best decisions. If nothing else, my staff will learn a great deal from the discussion."

"Your right, boss. It's about time I learned more about this cost stuff. I've played by their rules for so long now, what if they're wrong?"

Debbie and Tim nodded in agreement while Mary shot Jim a look that could kill.

Shut up Jim, thought Mike. "Maybe accounting will get a different perspective about costs."

"I doubt that," responded Fred. "But if we can clear up some things for your guys, maybe it's worth the time. Let's not drag it out though."

"I won't," said Mike as he took a deep breath and leaned back in his chair. It wasn't going to be easy. Fred was so insecure.

Mike was about to continue when Fred interrupted.

"You mentioned material only costing. What is that? Don't you mean a variable cost system?"

"I skipped a step and jumped right from a variable cost approach to material only costing, which is used by Lean companies."

"I've called other CFOs and controllers and I can't find another company doing Lean accounting. If it's so good, why can't I find anyone doing it?"

"Good question. I'll answer it after everyone un-derstands the alternatives."

"Why do we have to wait?"

"It'll be easier for everyone else that way."

"Come on, Fred, cut him some slack," said Jim.

"OK already!"

Mike continued. "Why do we, better yet, why does any company use a full absorption cost system?"

"Can someone tell me what a full absorption cost system is?" asked Debbie.

Mary responded. "Sure. With a full absorption cost system, all costs incurred in the manufacturing process are assigned to specific products. It sounds easy, and is in theory, but in practice it's difficult."

"Why?" asked Debbie.

"Because full costs include all material and labor used in production and all the other costs such as facility costs, your Purchasing department, manufacturing supervision, maintenance, etc."

"The Purchasing department gets charged to individual products? You mean the raw materials, don't you?"

"Raw materials are the easy part. It's easy to assign them to products based on the bills of material. The indirect costs—your salary, your staff's salary, travel, and supplies are also part of full manufacturing costs and have to be assigned to individual products. That's the challenge."

"I bet. I never thought about that. I'm just concerned with getting the right account numbers on the materials. When I see product costs on a computer printout I assume it's a straightforward calculation and it's accurate."

"It's anything but that. Costing is as much an art as a science."

"I'm starting to realize that now."

"Good. Let's get back to my explanation of a full absorption cost system. Assigning material to specific products is easy, but it gets more difficult with direct labor and it's extremely difficult with the overhead items."

"How's it done?" Debbie asked.

"What's with you Debbie? Why such an interest in costs?" asked Mary.

"It's simple. I've been in the middle of so many

disagreements between engineering and manufacturing about whether we should make or buy a part..."

"Disagreement!" yelled Jim from the back of the room. "Who you kidding? It gets nasty!"

"Jim, shut up and let me finish."

"Go ahead."

Everyone laughed. Debbie was probably the only one who could tell Jim to shut up without getting an earful. They worked together for a long time. Debbie was ten years older than Jim and, when he first joined Tricor, she took him under her wing like a younger brother.

Debbie continued, "I want to do what's best, but everyone has their own opinion on how our costs should be compared to purchase prices. If I understand how costs are calculated, I'll be able to help with the make vs. buy decision."

"That's for sure," responded Mary.

"It'll help me too," said Charles.

Everyone else nodded in agreement.

Mary continued. "Raw material's easy. What about direct labor?"

"I don't see what the big deal is about labor," said Charles.

"Good. Go ahead and explain it then," encouraged Mike, knowing full well that Charles would not be able to defend his process later on.

"Direct labor occurs when we change the form, fit, or function of the product."

"C'mon, we all know that," said Jim losing his patience.

"Will you sit down and relax?" responded Charles.

"Nope. Keep going, I'm listening."

"Our direct labor standards are developed by using a combination of theoretical and historical production rates and standard hourly rates. We estimate the annual output for an assembly area or machine based on standard manning levels to determine the standard labor cost per unit."

"Is it accurate?" asked Mike.

"Sure is," said Charles proudly in defense of his department.

"Mary, go ahead and finish up," said Mike.

"The last item in a full absorption cost system is overhead. Overhead's spread to individual products like labor is, but it's more complex."

"What do you mean?" asked Debbie.

"We calculate the annual overhead pool of expenses for all of manufacturing when we prepare our budgets each year. I'm in the middle of doing that now."

"Sounds like fun," quipped Jim. Debbie shot Jim another glance and he shut up.

Mary continued. "Overhead includes depreciation, utilities, manufacturing management salaries, property taxes, the cost of your Purchasing department, Debbie, and the other expenses that can't be assigned to individual products. Once we determine the overhead pool, we allocate the expenses to individual departments or work centers, based on specific rules for each item."

"What rules?" asked Tim.

"It's easier if I give you some examples. Property taxes and building depreciation are spread to work centers based on square footage. Management salaries and a lot of the other expenses are allocated to work centers as a multiple of direct labor."

"How?" asked Debbie.

"Say for example we have ten million dollars of overhead to allocate and five million dollars of direct labor in the work centers. We assign two dollars of overhead for each dollar of direct labor to "fully absorb" the anticipated overhead costs. Is everyone with me?"

"We're fine, go ahead," said Christy.

"In a full absorption cost system, the standard cost of a product consists of the material standards from the bills of material, the direct labor standards from Manufacturing Engineering, and overhead based on a multiple of direct labor for each operation of the manufacturing process. All manufacturing costs are assigned, one way or another, to every part we make or buy."

"That must take forever," said Debbie.

"Not really," replied Christy. "We've automated a lot of the routines and Mary just updates them each year."

"It's helped a lot, but it still takes too long. Overhead takes the most time."

"Why?" asked Charles.

"Think about it. Raw material costs are available anytime in the purchasing files, so that's not a problem. Direct labor's predictable based on historical data. But overhead's another story. Unless we have all the departmental spending forecasts, the capital plan, and detailed item-by-item production forecasts, assigning overhead's impossible. And we never get that data until the end of the budget process, so it's too late to update everything. It's a vicious cycle. We do the best we can."

"Is that why we have all those variances?" asked Jim.

"You got it," responded Mary.

"So why do we do it that way?" asked Debbie.

Fred jumped in, "The system's not perfect, but it's been good enough. We use full absorption for a number of reasons. First of all, it's required for GAAP."

"What the hell is GAAP?" asked Jim.

"That means Generally Accepted Accounting Principles. We wouldn't get a clean bill of health from our auditors at year-end if we didn't comply with GAAP. We also need to properly value our inventory for tax purposes, and a full absorption cost system provides a mechanism to assign all production costs to inventory. The IRS is interested in this as well."

"Why does the IRS care?" asked Jim

"Good question. If we don't properly allocate manufacturing costs to inventory, then the only alternative is to expense those items. That would lower our income and in turn reduce our income taxes. It's a significant tax issue and you can bet the IRS wants to collect every tax dollar it's entitled to."

"It always comes down to freakin' taxes. I don't need to know the specifics of the tax code, but let me see if I understand. The higher the cost of goods sold, the lower our income, the lower the taxes. So if we include all the overhead costs in our cost of goods sold, then at year end the cost of goods sold would be higher, our inventory would be lower, profits would be lower, and our taxes would be lower."

Mary looked in awe at Jim. "We have an opening in cost accounting if you're interested. You've been sandbagging us."

"I just want to know what the hell's going on."

"Yeah, right. Don't ask me for help anymore," responded Mary.

Everyone had a good laugh as Mary needled Jim. It took the edge off of the meeting.

"I want to make sure you all understand this," said Mary. "The IRS makes sure every item in inventory carries it's fair share of overhead, regardless of how many years it might sit there."

"Jim's a little ahead of me," admitted Charles reluctantly. "We either expense all of our overhead as it occurs, like we do with marketing & sales expenses, or we assign it to individual products. If we expense it right away, it lowers our earnings and our taxes. So the IRS insists we assign a portion of overhead to inventory."

"You explained it better then me."

Charles straightened up and smiled. "What's the IRS's rationale for doing this?"

"All assets of a firm have to be fairly valued on the Balance Sheet, and inventory's an asset."

"Got it," said Charles.

"It's about time," teased Jim.

Fred resumed his explanation of the benefits of a full absorption cost system. "There's one more reason we keep the current system. Our historical reporting, trend analyses, product pricing, and product development cost targets are based on standard costs we're used to. Changing methods would require a tremendous adjustment to our measurements."

"You did it," said Mike grinning from ear to ear."

"Did what? asked Fred.

"You answered your own question, why so few companies adopt Lean accounting. Inertia, or historical norms, are the major reasons everyone continues to use full absorption costing. It's true for most companies and that's why it's so difficult to find other firms using anything but a full absorption cost system."

"That may be one reason, but I also mentioned accounting and tax issues."

"I know you did, but you hit the nail on the head with your last comment. Changing a company's measurements is, in my opinion, the major obstacle to implementing Lean accounting. All the other reasons can be addressed, and more often than not, they're just excuses for avoiding change."

"Not so fast Mike. The accounting issues are real. And so is having valid benchmarks for decision making. We can't just abandon our measurements because you think Lean accounting's the way to go."

"I'm not suggesting we immediately abandon our current measures. We're just discussing the differences between traditional and Lean Accounting practices so we can make an informed decision. Whether we implement any changes, to what degree, and over what time frame can be discussed at a later point. I just want everyone to understand the choices."

"That's fine, as long as everyone realizes we're not

making changes until we understand the implications."

"Agreed. I don't want to hurt the business."

The room was quiet. Mike felt everyone wanted to hear more about Lean Accounting, but that wouldn't happen if he and Fred started to go at each other.

Mike continued. "Fred's brought up some excellent points. I don't understand your systems yet, so it's critical we decide what's best as a team. Maybe Lean Accounting or certain elements of it don't apply. That's a decision we'll have to make."

"That's my decision," stated Fred as he pushed his chair away from the table and threw his pen down.

"Sure it is. And it'll be a lot easier once we finish this."

Fred glanced at his watch. "I have another meeting soon."

"Let's try and wrap this up as quickly as possible," said Mike. "What about the problems of a full absorption cost system? I bet you thought of some while getting ready for this meeting. Debbie's already raised one issue."

"She sure has," responded Mary. "It's extremely time-consuming to maintain the allocation schemes each year, and we never quite finish. Some of our allocations haven't been adjusted in years."

"That's not unusual," said Mike. "It requires more overhead to keep up with the arbitrary allocation routines, and I haven't found a company yet that has the time, expertise, or methodology to accurately spread overhead costs to discrete products. There's no correct answer anyway. And what message does a full absorption cost system send to the manufacturing supervisors?"

Jim responded immediately. "That's easy. My variances are reviewed each month and I've learned how to beat the system..."

"As any seasoned supervisor has learned," said

Mike.

Jim continued, "the more direct labor hours we have, the more overhead I absorb, the lower my unfavorable overhead variance each month."

"Exactly. You have an incentive to produce labor hours, not product, to absorb overhead. You receive credit for anything produced, whether the customer ordered it or not. There's really no direct linkage between labor hours and customer demand."

"Wait a minute, that can't be true," said Scott. "It doesn't make any sense. Jim produces based on the forecast. He can't just go and produce anything he wants."

"C'mon Scott, get with the real world. You should spend some time out in the plant and see what really goes on," said Jim, laughing, from the back of the room.

"Long term, you're right Scott," said Mike, "but on a month-to-month basis, manufacturing has a lot of leeway. When necessary, I bet our supervisors produce a little extra to drive the monthly numbers. Why do you think so many companies are left with huge inventories when demand slows down?"

"Because the forecast stinks," blurted Scott.

"It always stinks," agreed Jim. "At least you understand that. There's hope for you yet."

"Lousy forecasting's only part of the inventory problem. It's our inability to rapidly turn off the spigot of incoming materials and production schedules that've been altered by supervisors that magnifies the problem. Inventories can explode in an MRP environment because everything changes so fast and no one can keep up with it. Besides, if supervisors are held accountable for overhead variances, they're forced to play the game and tweak the production schedule to their advantage."

"I've got to admit, we've been guilty of changing production to improve our numbers, but we don't do it much anymore. Fred knows we can't really influence the freakin' overhead variance. I wish he hadn't given us so much grief all these years."

Fred looked over the top of his reading glasses and glared at Jim.

"Sorry, Fred. But we used to have some pretty good battles..."

"C'mon, we haven't gotten on your case for quite awhile. Give us some credit," said Mary.

"It's gotten better, but you still have a ways to go. Besides, sales have been increasing, so it hasn't been much of an issue lately. Let's see what happens the next time we have a slow month."

"Based on my experience, overproducing to make the numbers is the rule, not the exception," said Mike.

"At least we're not the only ones fooling ourselves," said Scott.

"That was the case with all the companies I joined. It's hard to avoid when incentives reward production. Let me ask you this question then: who owns the overhead, or underabsorbed variance?"

"What do you mean, Mike?" asked Howard

"I mean, who's ultimately responsible for the overhead variance if we agree manufacturing doesn't really control it? Someone has to be responsible for it. After all, we determine those expenses annually based on the planned production schedule. If we don't produce to planned levels, we'll have an unfavorable overhead variance, so who's really responsible for it?"

"I never thought about it that way," responded Howard. "I guess sales is responsible since the only reason we wouldn't produce to planned levels, and therefore underabsorb overhead, is if planned sales didn't materialize."

"Hallelujah," said Jim. "That's what I've been thinking all these years. I'd get beat up about unfavorable variances and then leave the meeting scratching my head. I couldn't do anything about it. What the hell was I supposed to do, sell a building or stop paying property taxes? This is music to my ears. I can control the schedule and labor, but if we don't have enough demand, I can't do anything about overhead in the short term."

"Bingo!" said Mike. "In a Lean environment you wouldn't be allowed to produce anything just to make the numbers. There wouldn't be any over-or underabsorbed overhead variance calculations. That's all muda."

"How would you stop me from producing?" asked Jim.

"Since production takes place based on the pull of the customer, nothing can be produced unless a real order is received."

"Maybe for finished goods, but I'd still be able to make parts," pointed out Jim.

"No, you wouldn't," countered Mike. "Even within the plant, all production departments have customers, which are simply the next operation in the process. Using visual signals, or kanbans, each upstream work center receives a signal to produce only when the previous output has been consumed by the downstream operation. This eliminates the possibility of building excess inventory to absorb overhead."

"Sounds like a good theory, but how the hell can we operate like that?"

"It's radically different from traditional scheduling methods."

"Sure is. I can't imagine how we'd do that," commented Charles.

"A Lean plant would rather have equipment sit idle than produce on spec to absorb overhead and improve the monthly numbers," said Mike.

"That's a tough pill to swallow," said Jim.

"I know, but there's no guarantee the product will ever be sold. You're just gambling. Using full absorption and holding the plant responsible for overhead variances is inconsistent with Lean and sends conflicting messages to plant personnel. That's why it's so critical for accounting to change in tandem with manufacturing."

"Wow, I can see the problem now," said Mary. "It's beginning to make sense."

Everyone nodded except Fred. The more Mike's audience agreed with him, the greater the divide between him and Fred. Mike thought it was turning into a win/lose meeting and he wanted to avoid that at all costs. But he didn't have an answer to the dilemma, yet.

Mike also knew it was natural for Fred to be defensive. In a Lean implementation, department heads become painfully aware that they've been operating inefficiently for years, if not decades. It's hard to accept, especially so for Fred since he was so proud of his work.

Mike continued. "Another problem with the full cost approach is overhead expenses ultimately get to discrete products by 'riding the back' of labor."

"What do you mean?" asked Charles.

"As Mary said earlier, overhead's spread by determining a multiplier of direct labor for each department. So if a department has five thousand dollars of direct labor and you want to allocate ten thousand dollars of overhead to that department, the multiplier would be two. Multipliers range from a simple one-to-one ratio of overhead to direct labor to multipliers as high as ten-to-one. It can get ridiculous."

"How can it get so high?" asked Debbie.

"About sixty years ago, direct labor represented the bulk of the value-added component at a plant. Overhead was a relatively small portion of total spending, and spreading overhead based on labor dollars made sense. With the advent of automation, larger machines, and extensive staff to manage the systems, overhead now exceeds, and in some cases, dwarfs direct labor. Sixty-year old conventions don't work any more."

"We have some wild overhead rates here," said Mary. "Yesterday I was looking at a part that had five dollars of labor and twenty-five dollars of overhead."

"That happens all the time. Let's look at the alternative, a direct or, as some people call it, a variable cost system."

"It's obvious what that's all about," noted Jim, puffing his chest out a little. "Makes more sense to me already."

"Let me explain it for the benefit of everyone else," joked Mike.

"Can we take a freakin' bio break first, or isn't that allowed in Lean?" asked Jim.

"OK, let's take ten minutes."

During the break, Fred approached Mike. "I've been patient, but this is getting ridiculous. We need to wrap this up."

"We'll be done in half an hour, I promise."

"In half an hour, I'm out of here."

"Let's get going," said Mike to the group chatting just outside the conference room. He didn't want to waste a minute. They came in and took their seats and Mike continued. "With a variable cost system, only costs that vary as volume fluctuates are assigned to specific products. The remaining, or fixed costs, are managed in the aggregate. We switched to a variable cost system at my last three companies, and in each case we had much better information with lower maintenance, or upkeep, costs."

"But Mike, how can you have better information by tracking a smaller pool of costs?" said Tom. "That seems like a contradiction."

"It isn't. Let's discuss the benefits of a variable cost system and the answer will be obvious. Anyone have any ideas?"

Howard was the first to respond. "It'd make my life a lot easier."

"Why?" asked Charles.

"Each quarter, Mary and I update the forecast. We never have enough time, so we forecast the manufacturing variances with little input from the plant."

"I'll help. You just gotta ask," countered Jim.

"I know. Sometimes I just don't have the time. I wasn't criticizing you. Relax."

"I'm fine. Go ahead."

"To complete the forecast, I estimate the various costs, determine how much overhead, or as you call it, fixed costs, will be absorbed, and then calculate all of the variances. With volume fluctuations, it's tedious and error prone. If we had a variable cost system, I assume I'd just project the variable costs and variable margin by product line and overhead expenses in total."

"That's right," said Mike.

"And the variable margin would be more consistent as it wouldn't be affected by volume fluctuations, only product mix, which isn't a big issue here."

"Howard, you nailed that one. With a variable cost system, it's much easier to forecast results, especially when there are significant volume fluctuations. Variable costs also facilitate decision making, as incremental product costs are more visible. Can anybody else think of any benefits?"

"I sure can," said Mary. "It'll save a lot of time if I don't have to maintain all the allocation routines."

"You're right. All that time is muda. Instead we could use your help with value-added activity in the plant. We'll need a lot of nontraditional data collection for Lean and, unless we free up time by eliminating nonvalue-added work, we'll never improve."

Jim piped in. "If you eliminate overhead items on departmental statements, my guys will finally understand the numbers and take ownership for their results.

They want to do a good job but, just like in sports, they have to understand the scoring system. As much as we try, they just don't get it. Heck I don't always get it. This would be a big help."

"It'd help in purchasing, especially when I interface with Manufacturing Engineering," said Debbie. "They're always doing make/buy evaluations and, as I said before, we get confused as to what our real costs are. When we use fully absorbed costs, the buy alternative sometimes is more attractive, but then Jim objects if we outsource because he won't absorb overhead any more."

"Damn right," said Jim. "And the more you outsource the higher my unit overhead costs because now you have to allocate the same costs over lower production volumes. Seems like a vicious cycle that'll never end until the plant's empty."

"Come on Jim," said Fred, who had been stewing up to this point. "You know we try to remove the overhead components when we look at outsourcing alternatives. We do that to compare alternatives on an incremental cost basis."

"Let me tell you something, Fred, this comes up routinely and we don't have time to do a thorough analysis. It gets pretty confusing; especially when a manufactured part is routed through a number of work centers and each higher-level cost roll-up treats all previous level costs as material. It's damn near impossible to break out the overhead components for a complex product. If we involved accounting every time, Mary wouldn't get anything else done."

"I'll vouch for that," chimed in Charles. "It's not as easy as you think. Depending on who's making the argument, costs get interpreted differently."

Mike responded. "That's a real problem with a full cost system, especially if people don't know how to properly drill down and isolate true variable costs. It's much easier with a variable cost system. There's one other big benefit of a variable cost system."

"Yeah, what's that?" said Charles impatiently.

"A variable cost system isolates higher-level fixed costs so they can be managed more effectively. And over a short period, say a fiscal year, most overhead costs are relatively fixed."

"Now I'm confused," said Jim.

"Let me explain with an example that happened to me fifteen years ago and shaped my outlook on Lean accounting."

Mike had recounted this example at every company and could recite it in his sleep. But it got the point across.

"The incident occurred when I had my first assignment in manufacturing. I was the Chief Financial Officer of a heavy manufacturing company when the President asked me to become the VP of Manufacturing. I was responsible for a foundry that used electricity as the primary fuel source. The foundry was a few years old when we hired a consultant to implement a state-of-the-art cost system. From a financial point of view, the system worked perfectly. The consultant developed elaborate routines to track our key cost components: electricity, raw materials, and direct labor. All the items were discretely assigned to individual parts. In addition to material and labor variances, we had an electricity variance each month. During the first few months I was in charge of manufacturing, the system worked perfectly as all the cost components were "absorbed" by production and we had small variances. In the fourth month, volume was soft and the electricity variance went through the roof. Management immediately wanted to know what went wrong. Does anyone know what happened?"

Christy responded. "I bet electricity was really more of a fixed cost than a variable cost, and as soon as volume declined there wasn't enough production to absorb the electricity expense."

"You got it! Electricity was a fixed expense that should've been managed in a completely different manner. By treating electricity as a discrete product cost, no one "owned" this key expense, which was more than one million dollars a year, fifteen years ago. It was an overhead item that had to be managed over a nine -or twelve-month period, not daily or monthly as an item on the bill of material."

"Why nine months?" said Christy. "That seems odd."

"It is, unless you understand electricity billing. And no one understood it. We asked the power company to conduct an in-house seminar to explain their rate structure to our equipment operators and manufacturing engineers. Without getting into the details, the power company explained that there were many different rate periods; on peak, off peak, and, I think, intermediate peak periods. There was a usage charge and a demand charge as well. And each of these items changed, dependant on whether it was summer season or winter season. The most critical piece of information was that the demand charge, which was approximately half the bill, was determined by the maximum amount of power consumed in a single ten-minute period during the course of a month. We were obligated to pay at least eighty percent of this demand charge for the following nine months, whether the plant operated or not."

"So that's why you mentioned nine months."

"It was news to us. When the operators heard this, they were shocked. They asked all sorts of questions. They wanted to see when the peak demand period occurred. The power company passed out a graph showing that peak demand occurred daily from seven in the morning until ten past seven. Then someone asked the power company to examine each piece of equipment and determine its portion of peak demand. It was obvious that, as the plant started up each morning, four large machines were turned on at the same time and demand peaked."

"I know what I would've done," said Jim confidently.

"Let me finish."

"OK, boss."

"Within two days, the operators came up with a solution to save over three hundred thousand dollars a year by investing four dollars in light bulbs. The four operators running the largest pieces of equipment staggered their start times each morning, arriving at six thirty, six forty, six fifty, and seven o'clock. They started up their equipment when they arrived and, while in the start up mode, a red light on top of the machine would serve as a kanban, a visual signal to remind everyone that the other large pieces of equipment shouldn't be turned on. Each operator repeated this process in sequence until full start-up was achieved. It worked like a charm."

"I hope you gave them a big reward," said Jim.

"Boy, it figures that would be the first thing you'd think of," said Tom.

"They were taken care of," responded Mike. "More importantly, they felt great about their accomplishment. The point is, when you bury fixed or semifixed cost components in discrete product costs, you lose the ability to properly manage them."

"Ain't that true," agreed Jim.

"Also, fixed costs are determined by a completely different decision-making process. For example, depreciation is determined when the capital equipment purchase is approved. It doesn't matter how many parts are processed; the annual costs will be the same. Likewise for property taxes. These costs are set in stone when senior management selects the site for the plant. And finally, the costs for manufacturing management are only adjusted when processes materially change or significant volume fluctuations occur over some sustainable period. Loading these costs into discrete product costs sends, in my opinion, the wrong information to everyone."

"I can relate to that," said Mary. "At one of my previous companies the same thing happened. To further confuse the issue, the power company occasionally changed times for the on-peak and off-peak periods. It was like a game; we had to really stay on top of the issue or we'd get hosed."

"Good, so you know what I'm talking about."

"I see how we could benefit from excluding overhead in our product costs, but how's it done?"

"Let's hold off on the implementation issues, Mary. I'd like to let everyone think about what we've discussed. We've been at it long enough and I promised Fred we'd stop now."

"That's a good idea," said Tom. Everyone agreed except Fred.

"You haven't answered my question."

"I haven't forgotten. You still want to know 'Why aren't other companies adopting this approach?' And I haven't forgotten your question either, Jim, 'How can we have better cost information by tracking a smaller group of expenses?' I'll address them at our next meeting."

"But didn't you answer the first question already?" asked Mary.

"Not completely. Think about it."

The room was quiet. Everyone was absorbing Mike's comments. Mike was worried that they might be on overload and feared Fred would bolt at any time now.

"How long's this going to go on for? The budget will never get done if we're in meetings all the time.

We've been discussing this for almost a month now."

"Fred, please bear with me. We need to go through the two other elements of cost, direct labor and material, and we'll be done. It'll be a lot easier than discussing overhead. We need to understand this before we discuss the ramifications of possibly implementing Lean Accounting."

"Sounds like you've already made a decision."

"Absolutely not. I said we'd discuss it and see what applies here. Knowing how and where to apply Lean Accounting is a lot harder than just understanding it, and that's where your help and expertise are critical. It can't be done without you and your staff. Let's get through one more meeting and then we'll discuss further steps."

"One more meeting, but that's it. Set something up for next week and let's get this over with."

16 The Aftermath

After the meeting, the attendees gathered in small groups to debrief each other. Scott, Tom, Howard, Christy, and Mary gathered in Tom's office.

"Wow, Mike really knows cost accounting, doesn't he?" stated Mary. "It's neat to see it from a manufacturing perspective. He has some good ideas. I hope everyone keeps an open mind, especially Fred."

Tom responded. "Me, too, but Fred's still fighting everything. I know he's dead-set against Lean Accounting. It's really a shame because, if he cooperated with Mike, I think it'd be dynamite."

"I know what you mean," said Scott. "We just do the same things over and over again. This is our chance to learn something new. I suppose if I were close to retirement I wouldn't want someone telling me everything I've been doing for the last few decades is muda."

"It's gotta be tough on Fred. I feel for him," said Tom. "But I don't think Mike wants to change everything. Fred's too damn sensitive."

"I agree," said Mary. "Mike's trying not to offend Fred."

"Yeah, but he's doing a lousy job of it," interrupted Tom, and everyone agreed. "Once Mike gets on a roll, he's so passionate, he docsn't even realize he's criticizing Fred."

"Anyone in Fred's position would feel the same way. I certainly would," said Christy. "If he came on like that about IT, I don't think I could hold back either."

"I disagree," pointed out Tom. "IT's in a constant state of flux and you're used to change. It's a way of life for you. It's not like that in accounting."

"I never thought of it that way. I wish we could do something to help because I want to learn as much as I can from Mike. Fred's been great to us and I don't want him embarrassed in the process."

"But what can we do?" asked Howard. "Mike's worked at a number of places in both manufacturing and accounting, and has more experience than Fred. Fred's been at Tricor nearly his whole career and he feels threatened. He'll feel abandoned if he senses we support Mike."

"You're right. We have to make sure Fred knows we support him. If Lean's the right thing to do, he'll realize it."

Meanwhile, the manufacturing folks were huddling in Jim's office.

Charles was the first to comment.

"Boy, finally we have someone that can go toe-to-toe with accounting. Mike has some great ideas; I hope he'll get those bean counters off our backs for a change. They've been busting our humps for so long now, and for what? Their information's all wrong."

Jim responded. "Hold on. Mike wants to change things, but he doesn't want to alienate the rest of the company doing it. I had a long talk with him after the last meeting and he explained Lean only works if we're a team. He wasn't trying to piss off accounting. We're not going anywhere without their help, so don't get all excited about shoving their noses in the dirt. It's not in the cards."

Debbie agreed. "I learned a lot today and want to continue with Lean, but not at Fred's expense. It's a sensitive situation and Mike has to handle it carefully. It won't do anybody any good if we go around rubbing accounting's nose in it. Do you hear that, Charles? I know you butt heads with them all the time, but you have to back off now."

"I'll watch my P's and Q's. But I have to admit, I love to needle them."

"You'd better not. You'll ruin it for all of us."

Fred sat in his office contemplating his role in the Lean effort. He knew he had been very defensive, but he just couldn't stand how cocksure Mike was.

It was getting late and he decided he might as well head home. He was in no mood to get any work done at the office.

Fred walked into the house, set his briefcase in his office, and headed upstairs. As he passed through the kitchen, he ignored the stack of mail on the corner of the counter and barely acknowledged Sheila getting dinner ready. She knew she would hear all about it at dinner.

Ten minutes later Fred came downstairs, went to the refrigerator and poured a glass of wine, picked up the salad Sheila had prepared, and quietly sat down at the dinner table. Sheila joined him and wasted no time finding out what happened.

"Do you want talk or are you going to sit there and stew for awhile?"

Fred took a couple of sips of wine as Sheila anxiously waited for his response.

"It's the same old crap."

"Not Mike again. I thought you were beginning to like him."

"I was, but every time we have a meeting, I feel he's challenging my competence."

"Why, what does he do?"

"It's not exactly what he does, it's just that he makes it appear as if we've been doing things wrong all these years. My staff listens to him and they're hanging on his every word. It's obvious they like his ideas."

"You're feeling threatened again. I thought that after the luncheon meeting you felt more comfortable with him."

"I did. It's just the way he acts in the meetings. It makes me wonder."

"Do you still think he wants your position?"

"I don't know. He told me he left finance and accounting for manufacturing a long time ago and hasn't looked back. I know he loves this Lean stuff, and most of the Lean action is in manufacturing, so I think he's happy where he is."

"So why in the world would he be interested in your job?"

"I don't know, maybe to steamroll the Lean changes throughout the organization."

"Do you think he could steamroll your entire department?"

"Who knows?"

"Does he have time to devote to your area?"

"He managed accounting and manufacturing before, so he probably thinks he could do it again. He spends all his time thinking about this stuff."

"Tell him to get a life," said Sheila, hoping to calm Fred down. It didn't work.

"He's a jerk."

"Doesn't he need you and your staff to succeed?"

"I hope so."

"He's probably just trying to win everyone over."

"If that's what he's trying to do, he's no damn good at it."

"It seems to be working with your staff."

Fred put down his wine glass and snapped back. "What do you mean?"

"Do you really want to know?"

"Of course."

"Settle down, and I'll tell you. But you're not going to like it."

"Go ahead," said Fred as he tried to hide his frustration.

"It sounds like your embarrassed."

"What do you mean by that?"

"When you meet with Mike one-on-one, you get along fine. But when you and your staff get together with him, he irritates you. Maybe you feel like you're letting your staff down because you're not familiar with Lean Accounting."

"That's crap. I've been in finance and accounting for over thirty years and I know what I'm doing. Is it any different than when you come home upset because the Board of Education gave out new guidelines for Special Ed?"

"They do that all the time, and it gets me angry, but there's a big difference."

"Why's it different?"

"Because the new programs are unproven. We're always guinea pigs for their latest ideas to pacify the politicians, and the kids suffer."

"You're getting defensive now. Sounds like you don't like change either."

"Your situation's completely different. You told me Mike's approach has been successful at a number of companies; it's proven itself. I'd gladly change my lesson plans if the Board of Ed had a program that delivered results, but they don't."

Fred took another sip of wine and sat in silence. He didn't have a response for Sheila and started to shut down. Sheila had to keep the discussion going or Fred would finish the meal in silence.

"C'mon, stop having doubts about yourself."

"It's hard not to. I don't want my staff losing confidence in me."

"They won't. Give yourself a little more credit. How many companies are practicing Lean Accounting?"

"Hardly any."

"Good. You have an opportunity to be on the leading edge of your profession if you're willing to work with Mike."

"He's just so damn obnoxious!"

"He's probably not aware of what he's doing."

"If only that was the case."

"I bet it is."

"Even so, it's tough to get toward the end of my career and find out I could've been doing things a lot better all these years."

"Better to find out now, ahead of everyone else. It'll make your last few years at Tricor much more interesting. And don't tell me you don't welcome a challenge anymore."

"You know I do."

"If you show your staff you're open to new ideas, they'll continue to support you. They're young and eager to learn. You have more to lose if they see you being defensive."

"Maybe so."

"You've done it before. Didn't you embrace new computer systems twenty years ago, the Internet a few years ago, and a series of Presidents that threw everything at you."

"OK already. I get the point. Mike isn't the problem, it's me."

"It's both of you. You have to learn to trust each other."

"I hope you're right."

17 The Board's Demand

A few days later, Fred was at his desk when Peter called from the road.

"Fred, anything going on that I need to know about?"

"Not really. How are the meetings going?"

"That's why I'm calling. I want to make sure you haven't come up with anything that might affect the earnings forecast. I'm getting a lot of push back over the numbers."

"What else is new?"

"It's different this time. The Board and the analysts don't understand why we aren't making more headway with earnings growth, particularly since sales have been increasing. It's going to be a critical year and I wanted to double-check your forecast."

"Nothing's changed. Stick to the fifty-nine cents per share earnings figure. If we get lucky, we'll hit sixty cents, which is eight percent EPS growth. Take the heat now and you'll be the hero if we earn the extra penny."

"I doubt it. Everyone's clamoring for double-digit growth. The Board's running out of patience."

"They don't give a shit how competitive our industry is, do they?"

"C'mon, you know better. They could care less. The Board made it clear that we have to meet our projections. And Joe's expecting big improvements from manufacturing. Mike's initiatives better take hold by the end of the year. Speaking about Mike, how are you two doing?"

"I had another grueling session with him."

"You told me the relationship had improved."

"It may've been my fault."

"What happened?"

"Peter, it's not easy to admit this, but it's hard to have some young guy come in and explain how everything needs to change. The thought of his being right is hard to accept."

"That's the way it is with Lean, not just for accounting, but for every area of the company, including me. How do you think I feel, especially with Joe telling me what to do?"

"I hadn't thought about that."

"That's why Lean usually doesn't get started until a company's on the verge of going out of business or new management's brought in."

"What do you mean?"

"If you're going under, you'll try anything. And with new management, they're not wedded to the past, so there's little resistance to change."

"I see."

"So get used to change. I've spoken with enough companies to know that Lean's critical to our long-term survival. And we can't do it without you."

"I'm trying to work with Mike, it's just so difficult."

"It's the right approach for the company. Forget about past practices and use your considerable intellect to evaluate Mike's proposed changes. I'm confident you'll see the benefits. I have to go now. See you in a few weeks. We can wrap up the budget then."

"You bet."

After hanging up, Peter called Mike.

"Mike, it's Peter, how are things going?"

"Fine, how's your trip?"

"The meetings are going well. I just spoke with Fred. He's going to be a tough convert. He's having trouble with the changes you're proposing."

"I know. No matter what I do, I can't convince him about the merits of Lean."

"Lean's not the problem. He's questioning his competence. You have to handle this very carefully. He's a key player, and I rely on him a great deal."

"I'm trying my best not to offend him. He's so defensive that sometimes he comes off looking foolish in front of his staff. I thought I patched everything up, but the last meeting was rough. I could tell he was feeling down even though his staff was getting excited about the changes."

"He doesn't want to lose the respect of his staff. You're the new guy with the radical ideas and they'll gravitate to you, especially when you demonstrate such a grasp of their area of expertise. Don't let that happen."

"I'm trying. But Fred's got to work with me. He can't be defensive about everything."

"He's trying. Keep me up-to-date on the situation."

"Will do. Good luck with the rest of your trip."

"Thanks."

Mike put the receiver down and thought about the last meeting. He wondered if he could've done anything differently.

18 Inventory Write Down

Mike headed to Debbie's office to see how she was doing with the electronic kanban initiative. Mary joined them to review the initial data.

"Debbie, have you had any discussions with the suppliers yet?" asked Mike.

"Sure have. I spoke with both of them this week and they're open to the idea, but they're skeptical. They had all sorts of questions."

"Like what?"

"How would they know what quantities to deliver, who bears the cost of more frequent deliveries, what commitments would we provide for work in process at their plants, what are the specific billing and payment procedures, etc. We need to meet with them."

"I know. Invite them in so we can explain the details. Their questions are natural, and fortunately easy to address."

Turning toward Mary, Mike continued. "What were the results of your analysis?"

"The two suppliers we selected provide us with about ninety different parts."

"Good. That's enough to give us a feel for how this'll work. How much do we spend with them?"

"About five million dollars. That's five percent of our annual material purchases."

"Are the parts representative of the total inventory?"

Inventory Write Down

"Absolutely. The ninety parts turn four times per year, which parallels our overall inventory turns."

"Great. That'll give us a heads-up on what we can expect as we add more and more parts to Nocturne."

Debbie chimed in. "I always hear accounting discussing inventory turns and working capital management. What exactly does it mean?"

"I'm glad you asked. Inventory turns measures the speed at which a company uses the components of a product. It can be calculated in dollars, in which case turns equals the annual cost of sales of the parts in question divided by the average inventory value of those parts. Alternatively, you can divide the total number of parts shipped during the year by the average number of parts kept in inventory. Either way we'd arrive at the same answer. Since we're turning these parts four times per year, we have about a three-month supply on hand. If we didn't order more parts and sales remained the same, it'd take ninety days before we'd run out.

"That sounds easy enough."

"You think so?" said Mike with a grin. "I usually explain inventory turns to the entire workforce with an example everyone can relate to—grocery shopping. I do the grocery shopping for my family once a week. Can you equate that to inventory turns Debbie?"

"Sure, if you go once a week then you're turning your grocery inventory fifty two times a year."

"Not so quick. Assume I start with an empty refrigerator each week and completely refill it with each shop. What would the average inventory be?"

"Oh, I get it now," said Debbie, slightly embarrassed that she fell for Mike's trick. "On average there'd be one-half of a week's groceries in the refrigerator."

"Right. So what are the turns?"

"One hundred and four."

"Bingo! Think of all the problems you'd have if you only turned your groceries twelve times a year, or only four times a year like we do. Your obsolescence would be enormous, you wouldn't be able to find anything, and you'd need to buy a few more refrigerators. It's no different in business."

"That's a good example. Does everyone immediately think it's fifty-two turns?"

"Just about. I wonder if Mary fell for it."

"You'll never know," said Mary with a sly smile and a wink at Mike.

"How about working capital, what's that?"

"Working capital, at the most basic level, consists of inventory, accounts receivable and accounts payable. They're assets and liabilities of the company that'll generate or consume cash in a relatively short period, certainly less than a year. It's very important for a firm to manage its working capital, and from what I've heard, it's been a challenge here because of difficulties in manufacturing."

"How's it measured?"

"Let me give you an example." Mike went to the white board and drew some timelines. "On average we pay our suppliers thirty-five days after we receive the materials. We collect our money from our customers about fifty days after the product's shipped. In between, materials sit in our inventory for about ninety days, since inventory turns four times per year. Our working capital investment is one hundred and five days, (90 days plus 50 days minus 35 days). It takes a hundred and five days from our initial cash outflow until we collect from our customers. It's a significant cost, and with Lean we should significantly reduce this investment."

"Let me see if I understand," said Debbie. "I don't want to get tricked again with a quiz."

"Go ahead."

"If we received raw materials today, we'd pay for them in 35 days, ship product to our customers, on average, 55 days after that, and then collect from our customers 50 days after shipment. So we'd have to finance this activity for 105 days."

"Bingo!"

"That must get expensive."

"It sure does. That's why most manufacturing companies take out working capital lines of credit."

"But won't Lean just reduce the turns portion of the equation?" asked Debbie.

Mary responded. "Normally that'd be true. But one reason it takes so long to collect from our customers is that we hardly ever ship complete orders. And customers look for any reason to delay payment. We give them a great excuse."

"Shouldn't they at least pay for what they received?"

"You'd think so, but that's not the way it works. Our customers can't pay us, or so they claim, since in many cases they can't collect from their customers for the same reason. So until we improve the manufacturing and delivery process and ship complete orders, our collection efforts won't improve."

"That's one of the reasons Lean's so powerful," said Mike. "It improves two parts of the equation, inventory turns and collections. By improving production flows, inventory declines, order-fill rates improve, and collections accelerate. You can double inventory turns during the first few years of a Lean implementation. That's why Lean's such a great cash generator."

"But didn't you mention that we'd ask the suppliers for early pay discounts if we pay in only 10 days? Wouldn't that defeat what we're trying to achieve?" asked Debbie.

"You're right, early pay discounts will accelerate our cash payments to our suppliers by twenty-five days, but the return on that investment is tremendous. Fortunately, the reduction in inventory will fund the early pay program. And besides, early pay discounts are op-tional; Lean's just making it easier by generating the cash."

"Thanks, I finally understand working capital."

"I'm glad you're asking these questions. It's important to understand the entire process. Now let's get back to Mary's data on the sample parts."

Mary resumed her explanation. "The ninety parts that'll be in the kanban program are turning four times a year, but that's a group average."

"Is that a problem?" wondered Debbie.

"It might be. In any group we have parts that turn much faster than the average and we have the real laggards. I'm concerned because we have some parts that haven't even moved in a year."

Mike inquired, "Doesn't the company have an inventory obsolescence reserve to address the slow moving parts?"

"Of course, but the reserves are calculated by part groupings. We never have the time or systems capability to drill down to the individual part number. The point is our inventory obsolescence reserve may not be sufficient."

"Aren't you jumping to conclusions?" asked Debbie.

"Not really. The parts I investigated account for about one and a quarter million dollars of inventory. If I applied our inventory obsolescence formula to these parts as a group, we'd have an inventory reserve of about eighty thousand dollars, or about seven percent."

"And you don't think that's enough?" asked Mike.

"I know it's not. I analyzed each part and took into account additional information such as discontinued items that haven't been coded in the system yet, trend data on slow-moving items that don't look bad now, but in reality will become a big risk, and the obsolescence reserve should be about a hundred and twenty-five thousand dollars."

"Wow, that's a big difference," noted Debbie.

"It doesn't surprise me," said Mike calmly. "As a company lowers its inventory it exposes all sorts of problems, one of which is inventory obsolescence. The fact that there's more 'garbage' in inventory than we realized becomes apparent. It was always there; we just didn't know it nor did we have an incentive to uncover it. Have you discussed it with Fred yet?"

"No, I wanted to review it with you first to see if I was correct. The forty-five thousand dollar obsolescence difference isn't a big deal by itself, but that was for only five percent of our inventory. If this pattern holds up over the entire inventory we're looking at a nine hundred thousand dollar write-down."

"That's not bad," said Mike.

"What? How can it be good news?"

"Believe me, it is. At my previous companies, the inventory 'surprise' was always a much, much bigger percentage than you've uncovered. It also means your reserve techniques are better than most. I just hope these parts mimic what we'll find with the rest of the inventory."

"They better," said Mary. "Fred hates surprises, especially when they expose flaws in the financial systems."

"It's perfectly normal, he has to understand that."

"Not a chance. He takes too much pride in his reporting; he'll think he messed up."

"The inventory write-down will get worse than your preliminary calculations. When you go from ninety days of inventory to, say, forty-five days and then to world class levels of seven days, you'll always find a lot more suspect inventory along the way. You'd never uncover the problem with computer-generated models. In all my years in business, no matter what inventory reserve model was employed, I've never seen a favorable inventory adjustment as inventory levels were reduced. I think it's a natural law of the universe. Let's keep our fingers crossed it's only nine hundred thousand dollars."

"I hope it doesn't get any worse."

"Enough about obsolescence. Tell me about the work you did on the kanbans."

"Sure," said Mary. "I used the kanban formulas you gave me and it looks like we won't be ordering much material for the next couple of months."

"That's usually the case," acknowledged Mike.

"Once we work off the excess inventory, we'll only have about six hundred and fifty thousand dollars of inventory, and that's before we start reducing the number of kanbans from the initial levels. It was an eye opener."

Mike was getting excited as Mary was starting to see the financial power of Lean. He continued. "As we get better with Lean, inventory will continue to decrease. We'll have to work with the suppliers as well as adjust some internal processes before we push it too far."

Mary turned to Debbie, "What's the matter, you don't seem too happy about this?"

"Before you both get too excited, we have to convince the suppliers to participate. I imagine that'll be my responsibility."

"That makes sense," said Mary. "What's the problem?"

"I can't wait to tell them that we won't be placing orders for the next few months since we'll be reducing our inventory. You really know how to paint a pretty picture."

"There's lot's of benefits for the suppliers," responded Mike.

"Like what?" she snapped back."

"They'll benefit by having more visibility into our consumption, by eliminating discrete purchase orders and invoicing, by reducing their inventories and their risk of obsolescence, and by reducing expediting and cancellations."

"They'll still be skeptical."

"Of course they will. Invite the two suppliers in and I'll review the entire process with them."

"Good. We'll see how smooth you are," said Debbie, grinning from ear to ear. "I'll schedule the meetings for next week."

"Let me warn you about one other thing."

"What now?" groaned Debbie.

"We'll need to consolidate our supplier base."

"Why?"

"It's too difficult to implement all these changes with a large supply base."

"That's not going to be easy. We need all of them."

"Not really. We'll concentrate on the best suppliers and offer them more business if they go along with the changes."

"It's not that easy. We didn't get all these suppliers just to make our lives difficult. We need them."

"Everyone says that, but it's not true. You'll see for yourself."

"I hope you're right."

"It won't happen over night. It'll be a slow, steady process."

Mary turned toward Debbie, "Sounds like you'll have your hands full just like accounting. Mike's an equal opportunity pain in the ass..."

"Now wait a minute. You'll thank me for this in a couple of years."

"A couple of years," gasped Debbie. "I hope we see some benefits long before that."

"You will. I guarantee it."

"Now we can rest easy," said Mary as she struggled to hold in her laughter.

"If I wasn't so concerned, I'd be laughing also," said Debbie.

"That's enough already," said Mike. "Let's move on. How's IT doing? Have they coordinated everything with the software provider?"

"Well, that's another issue," responded Mary. "They're overloaded. This was never on their schedule. You'll have to talk to Fred to get the resources needed to implement the server, load the software, and enter the initial data for the ninety parts."

"Great, but should I talk to him before or after you tell him about the nine hundred thousand dollar inventory problem, Mary?"

"C'mon, that wasn't called for. The last thing anyone wants from the financial area is a surprise, and Fred's worked hard to develop routines to accurately predict financial performance. If you make changes that have an impact on the financials, you have to warn us in advance. We can't anticipate the impact of Lean. You know it's all new to us."

"You're right. I'll go with you to see Fred."

"Thanks, just don't piss him off."

"I won't."

Mary and Mike headed down to Fred's office.

"I know I'm not the easiest guy to work with, but I really don't mean to cause any problems for Fred."

"So why are you so impatient with accounting?"

"Truthfully, because accounting's usually a huge roadblock to a speedy Lean implementation and it frustrates the hell out of everybody in manufacturing."

"Do you think you may have something to do with it?"

"I expected you to say that. I know it's not me because I hear it from almost all of my buddies in manufacturing. It's always a topic of conversation at Lean meetings."

"Why does everyone think we're a roadblock?"

"Because accounting's against change. Lean initiatives affect financial results and the methodologies used to track performance in manufacturing. And when accountants find themselves in unfamiliar territory, they resist."

"Well, if we don't understand something, you can't expect us to blindly go along. We have to maintain the integrity of the financial reports."

"Exactly, and that's why I'm trying to explain all of this by going through the detail with accounting. It's painful, but it's the only way to learn it."

"Does it really have to be painful?"

"I'm doing the best I can. And I'm going to need your help more than anyone."

"Why me?"

"Because cost accounting undergoes the most radical change. I'll also need your help dealing with Fred. He has a great deal of respect for you."

"I want to help. It'll be a challenge to use some different techniques in the financial area. But trust me, it'll go a lot smoother if you can just figure out how to get Fred's support. He's a smart guy and wants to buy into the changes, and he has to be part of the team to make it work. You need to find a way for him to have a meaningful role."

"I need to figure that one out. In the meantime, I don't want to create a bigger rift between Fred and me with this inventory issue. Any ideas?"

"We're basically telling him the current reserve methods aren't correct. He's not going to like that."

"I know. But every manufacturing company in the world has this problem. Overall averages suffice and the auditing companies buy off on it. The only time inventory finally gets cleaned up is when there's a change in top management or a sale of the company. Then every possible bit of bad news is immediately recognized on the financial statements so that new management maximizes its probability of success."

"Are you suggesting we're intentionally hiding something?"

"Not at all. It's hard to get into this level of detail until inventory's dramatically lowered, and then the problems surface. And it's hard for existing personnel to disclose large inventory discrepancies and the associated hit to the Income Statement. It'll be embarrassing for Fred, there's no denying that."

"Peter and the Board of Directors must realize this'll happen during a Lean implementation."

"Let's hope so."

Mike hesitated for a second as he collected his thoughts. "Let's not discuss this with Fred right now. I just thought of a better way to explain it. I'll tell you later."

"If I'm off the hook that's fine with me. Just don't let it drag out. We're expected to bring bad news to Fred as soon as it's uncovered."

"I'll explain it to Fred tomorrow. I promise."

Mike started to walk away and Mary grabbed his arm. "Don't screw it up, OK." He nodded and headed down the hall.

19 Bad News Again

The next morning Mike had his Administrative Assistant track down Peter.

"Hi, Peter, it's Mike. I hope I'm not out of line tracking you down."

"Not at all. What can I do for you?"

"I thought you'd be able to help me with a problem."

"I'll try. What's it about?"

"I've been working with Purchasing and Accounting to establish an automatic replenishment system with our suppliers. Once implemented, we'll be able to significantly lower inventory levels."

"That's great, so what's the problem?"

"Our inventory obsolescence reserves are insufficient."

"How do you know that?"

"To set up the kanbans, we examined about five percent of total inventory in excruciating detail and, according to Mary, we potentially have a million-dollar inventory write-down."

"Just what we need now. How confident is she?"

"She's pretty sure. The sample's representative of the entire inventory."

"What do you think?"

"Based on my experience, our system's better than most. The surprise could've been a lot worse."

"What do you mean, it could've been a lot worse?

I just gave the Board a forecast update and now you spring this on me. What do you think this will do to our credibility?"

"Didn't the Board warn you about this? It's pretty typical."

"It never came up."

"Damn, I'm sorry I didn't warn you earlier. I didn't think it would happen so soon. And I guess I was hoping we'd be the exception to the rule."

"Sounds like my beef's with the Board, not you. I hope you didn't just drop this bomb on Fred's lap."

"No, I didn't."

"Good. Are you sure it's a million dollars?"

"It's our best estimate for now. I wanted to let you know as soon as we discovered it."

"Thanks. Unfortunately, it'll have a significant effect on our earnings per share. How long will it take to nail down the exact number?"

"It'll be awhile. We're experimenting with a sample of parts for three to six months to test the new process before we expand the kanbans. Also, these items represent five percent of inventory dollars, but only two percent of the inventory items. It's a lot of work to examine the rest of the SKU's and it's not in our plans right now."

"We'll have to take the earnings hit this quarter. I'll discuss it with Fred."

"I was hoping you'd do that."

"I'll also have to let the Board know right away. They're already clamoring for earnings growth. A million-dollar inventory hit will lower earnings by more than two cents a share."

"How big a problem is that?"

"I'll find out soon enough. They want earnings growth and we haven't delivered yet."

"I'm glad I don't have to deal with that. What do you suggest I tell Fred?"

"Tell him what you found and let him know that you already discussed it with me. I'll take it from there."

"Thanks. I'll discuss it with him as soon as we're finished."

"Good. I'll make sure I'm available to take his call. Thanks for letting me know."

Mike hung up the telephone and headed down to Fred's office.

Fred was engrossed in his work when Mike knocked on the open door. Fred looked up and couldn't hide his less-than-enthusiastic reaction to Mike's presence. He signaled Mike to enter.

"Do you have a few minutes?"

"What are you up to?"

"We're developing an automatic replenishment program with our suppliers and we had to examine some inventory items in detail."

"I don't like the sound of this. I hope you don't have any bad news."

"Unfortunately, I do. The inventory reserve isn't big enough to cover the additional obsolescence we'll uncover as we lower inventory levels."

"Has Mary been involved?"

"Absolutely, she made the calculations."

"How big's the problem?"

"About a million dollars."

"Shit! Are you sure? Our auditors always accepted our reserve calculations."

"C'mon, with over forty million dollars in inventory, there's no way you can estimate the exact amount of the reserve. We all know it's just a best guess, and so do the auditors."

"For once we agree. So why do you think your estimate is any better?"

"As we implement Lean and reduce inventory we'll continuously uncover problems. It's happened at all the other companies I worked for."

"That's no damn consolation."

"It should be. The potential write-down as a percent of inventory is by far the lowest I've seen. There's nothing wrong with your methods."

"Thanks, but it doesn't make me feel any better. I'll need to tell Peter about this."

"I already made Peter aware of the problem."

"You did what?" exclaimed Fred as he stood up and slowly walked over to the window.

"We spoke just before I came down to tell you."

"Why the hell did you tell Peter before me?"

"Because the write-down's normal during a period of inventory reduction, and I wanted Peter to know that."

"So how'd he react?"

"Not too bad. You'll find out when you talk to him."

"You bet I will."

"I have one other item to discuss."

"More bad news?"

"I need help from IT to install the online kanban system."

"You're kidding! How am I going to free up resources in IT at this time of year? We're buried!"

"It won't take much time. We're using the ASP model I demonstrated."

"I don't care what model you're using, we don't have time."

"Hear me out. We just need to install some equipment, load the necessary software, provide links to our web site and initialize the data. It won't take more than two or three days."

"It's never that easy. Who you kidding?"

"It is. I've done it before. We've gotta get this going ASAP."

"What's the rush?"

"If Peter's going to explain the inventory write-down as a byproduct of new manufacturing strategies, we need to improve inventory turns, and soon. And once we get it going we can take advantage of early pay discounts, which will be funded by the reductions in inventory."

Fred buried his head in his hand and grimaced. "I guess I don't have a choice. Let me talk to Christy and we'll see what we can do."

"Thanks."

"Anything else, or should I just make an entry on my calendar for the weekly bad-news update from you?"

"Don't get so down over this. There's nothing you could've done to prevent it. I've often thought that if the worldwide manufacturing community cut inventories magically by fifty percent, the total obsolescence reserve would increase by trillions of dollars. It's there, but it's invisible."

"I get the message, but it still bothers me."

"I understand. But let's move on. Can we wrap up the discussion on cost system alternatives tomorrow?"

Fred returned to his chair and his five-foot ten-inch frame slowly collapsed into the worn seat. He took a deep breath and hesitantly said, "Before we talk about the meeting, there's something I need to ask you."

"Sure, go right ahead," said Mike as he pulled up a chair.

"You've been spending a lot of time with my staff, especially Mary, and it seems as though you've decided to redesign the entire accounting system with or without my approval. Are you trying to speed up my retirement?"

"Absolutely not."

"That's hard to believe."

"C'mon Fred. I've been out of finance and accounting so long now, why would I want to go back? I'm having too much fun in manufacturing. And besides, for the most part we've only been discussing cost accounting, which is just a small part of your responsibility."

"I figured that was just the beginning."

"No way! If it'll make you feel any better, let me give you the names and phone numbers of the CFOs and Controllers I've worked with at my last two companies. Get their viewpoint. It'll carry more weight than anything I might say."

"I'd like to do that."

"Good. I'm glad you finally told me what was bothering you. I know a Lean transformation is difficult, and believe me, I want to work with you, not against you."

Mike took out his Palm Pilot and looked up the phone numbers, wrote them on a piece of paper, and handed them to Fred.

"Maybe I've overreacted."

"You have. Talk to my references, it'll put the issue to rest once and for all."

"I hope so."

"Now, can we continue with the meetings?"

"Sure, we're ready. And, if your references confirm what you've told me, then expect a serious attitude adjustment on my part."

"I'm looking forward to it. See you at nine in the conference room."

As Mike left Fred's office, he stopped, turned toward Fred and said "Just one more thing. I'll be conducting our first 5S event in the shop and I'd like to have someone from your area on the team."

"Boy, you never quit, do you?"

"Can't afford to if we want to move ahead."

"How much time do they have to commit?"

"An event takes three days and it's important that all team members participate for the entire event."

"It seems like there's no end to the time requirements for Lean."

"I wish I could magically snap my fingers and complete the transformation, but that's not possible. It's a lot of hard work. That's why so few companies are willing to stay the course."

"Let me get back to you."

"Great, see you tomorrow."

Mike left and Fred dialed Peter's cell phone.

"Hello."

"Hi, Peter, it's Fred."

"I've been expecting your call. Mike told me about the inventory problem."

"He just left my office. How big a problem do you think it'll be with the Board?"

"It's a problem, that's for sure, but I'm more concerned that Joe didn't warn me."

"Do you think he's up to something?"

"I hope not. If he has a problem, he usually let's me know it. I'll give him a call."

"Let me know if I can help."

"Sure will. And by the way, Mike was surprised the write-down was so small."

"Really. Thanks for telling me."

"I've gotta run now."

Fred thought about the conversation. He was relieved with the way Mike handled the situation. If Mike had been trying to undermine him, this was the perfect opportunity. By conveying the bad news directly to Peter, Mike had taken the pressure off. Fred planned to be more supportive of Mike's recommendations, provided the references corroborated Mike's comments.

20 Thanks Joe

"Hello."

"Hi, Joe, it's Peter."

"How you doing?"

"Seems we have a problem. Mike just told me we'll have a million dollar inventory write-down."

"How come?"

"While setting up the kanban program, he discovered our obsolescence reserves are too low. Why didn't you warn me and the Board about this?"

"I was going to talk to you when we finalized the budget. I thought it'd be awhile before we'd have to deal with this, if at all. I was hoping we were fully reserved—I know how conservative Fred is."

"Well, it's a problem, and I understand it's not unusual."

"It depends on your reserve policy. In any event, we'll need to make it up somehow. We have to hit the earnings forecast. The Board's counting on it."

"I'll see what we can do."

"Let me know if I can help."

"Thanks."

That son of a bitch, thought Peter. He knew it all along.

21 Reference Checks

There was still enough time left in the day to contact Mike's references. Fred wanted to talk with Mike's former colleagues before the next meeting. He called the first reference, Jack Harris, the CFO of Advance Electronics. Fortunately, Mr. Harris's secretary said Jack would take his call.

Fred began, "Jack, I'm Fred Chapman, the CFO at Tricor Electronics. Do you have a few minutes to discuss Mike Rogers, our Manufacturing Vice President?"

"Sure, anything I can do to help. Mike really gave my career a boost."

"Really? That's what I want to discuss. He has a lot of new ideas for our manufacturing group, but it seems like he wants to change a lot of other areas as well."

"That's Mike all right. He did the same thing at Advance and it caught most of us off guard. Initially, I hated the guy."

"Boy, that sounds familiar!"

"He's at it again, I assume."

"Sure is."

"Don't let it bother you. When he came to Advance, I was the Controller, so he really made an impact on my area. His people skills were, shall we say, less than stellar. At first I thought he was crazy, but it didn't take long to realize he was going to have a huge positive impact on the company."

"Really, how so?"

"Once he started to implement his Lean program, our productivity soared, our inventory turns went up by fifty percent, and customer service levels were the best ever."

"That's great."

"It didn't happen immediately, but once Lean got going, progress built upon itself. It was Mike's first attempt to lead the transformation and he had to learn to work with his peers. That was his only weakness. After he left Advance he had a lot of success at his next company."

"Mike's been here a few months and we've had our differences. He has strong opinions about accounting practices and it's unnerving. I was beginning to wonder if he had any ulterior motives, so he suggested I contact you."

"I'm glad you did. I owe Mike a lot. By working closely with him, I learned a great deal about simplifying accounting routines while providing more value-added support to the manufacturing group."

"He talks about that all the time."

"I know. And he's right. He changed my perspective on accounting. In fact, my success supporting Lean played a large part in my promotion to CFO at Advance."

"So he had no interest in taking over your department?"

"Hell no. Why would he? He loves what he's doing."

"But he wants to change everything I'm doing."

"That's Mike, aggressive as hell, but that doesn't mean he wants to take over accounting. He just needs your support."

"That's what he says."

"It's true. I'm surprised he hasn't improved his interpersonal skills after all these years. You can tell him

I said that."

"He's like a bull in a china shop. It's difficult to give him the benefit of the doubt."

"He's really a good guy. You'll learn a great deal from him. I certainly did."

"I'll try to be more patient with him."

"One piece of advice. Mike's programs will free up a lot of capacity and cash. The pressure will be on you, and your CEO, to find acquisition candidates to utilize the facility and people. It's never too early to start thinking about that."

"Thanks for the advice. It was a pleasure talking to you."

"Glad I could help. One more thing. If you want to shut Mike up, ask him about the employees he lost in Boston."

"What do you mean?"

"Just tell him I told you to ask about it."

"I won't forget. You've got me curious now."

"Good luck."

"Thanks again."

Fred contacted the other references and received similar feedback. Working with Mike was difficult at first, but in each instance, led to great results and career advancement. Fred was relieved after the last conversation and promised himself he would support Mike from this point forward.

That evening Fred shared this new information with Sheila. She did all she could to hold back the "I told you so's." They had a great dinner, shared a bottle of wine, and looked forward to three exciting years at Tricor.

22 Round Three

Once again the group was gathered in the Board Room to review traditional cost systems vs. Lean Accounting. The previous meeting focused on the relevancy of allocating overhead costs to discrete products. Now it was time to discuss labor and material reporting.

Mike opened the meeting.

"We'll try to wrap up the discussion of different costing methodologies today. Before we discuss labor reporting, does anyone have any questions about overhead reporting?"

"Just a comment," said Mary. "I've been thinking about our discussion of manufacturing overhead, and basically you're suggesting we treat this expense like the S, G & A (Selling, General and Administrative) expense of the entire company."

"Exactly, they're the G & A expenses of manufacturing. I would go a little deeper though."

"What do you mean?" asked Mary.

"We should try to assign the overhead as best as possible to discrete product families or groupings."

"Why?" asked Scott.

"Because we still want to know if we're making money at the product family level. I'd also try to incorporate the company-wide S, G & A into the product family Income Statement. If it can be done easily, fine; if not, we're no worse off."

"I can see where product family Income Statements wouldn't be much of a problem, but only if we examined the business at a fairly high level," said Mary.

"That's the only place it's relevant, Mary. As you drill down deeper and deeper, the information becomes less and less accurate, with the exception of material costs. Now, let's move on and discuss direct labor."

Fred interrupted. "Mike, I can guess where you're headed with this. Are you suggesting we treat direct labor like overhead and not track it in detail?"

"Absolutely. Great observation! Direct labor reporting has the same problems as overhead, and the problems are magnified in a Lean environment."

At this suggestion, not only were the accounting folks becoming uncomfortable, but so were the manufacturing managers, particularly Jim and Charles. Mike would have to convince the entire room of the merits of this change, but that wasn't any different from his previous Lean transformations.

Mike continued, "To understand why we might want to consider eliminating labor reporting, let's review the questions from our first meeting. Mary, did you get a chance to work up any of the answers?"

"Sure did. Direct labor's only fifteen percent of costs."

"How stable was it?"

"I plotted direct labor expenses for the past twenty-four months and was surprised to find out that it was relatively constant, despite volume fluctuations." Mary handed out some graphs and continued, "As you can see in these graphs, month-to-month total labor spending was constant, even when volumes declined, as typically happens in the summer months."

"So what do you make of this?"

"Our direct labor really doesn't change within certain volume bands, at least in the short run."

"Correct, and based on what happens in the summer months, how wide are those bands?"

"Looks like about twenty-five percent."

"You're going through a lot of work to track labor to discrete products and forecast variances, and you just proved it's a fairly fixed expense, within wide volume bands. You also said direct labor's fifteen percent of total product costs, which means it's only nine percent of total expenses. Nine percent isn't very significant, especially when you consider how much time and effort is spent measuring direct labor. Did you research the costs to maintain the labor reporting system?"

"Sure did. It costs about a half million dollars per annum on the plant floor. And that doesn't include administrative or manufacturing engineering costs to maintain the system."

"That a lot of money. Does everyone in the room use the reports?"

"My supervisors look at the reports every day, but they usually complain there's some gamesmanship going on with the way employees assign their labor," responded Jim.

Charles added, "My engineers spend quite a bit of time maintaining and correcting the routings so the system's up to date, but we're forever behind. It's impossible to keep up with the changes."

"Jim, do you think the reports are accurate?" asked Mike.

"Not really."

"Why?" asked Fred.

"On the assembly floor we move people from department to department based on schedule changes and material availability, and we don't have enough time to make sure the labor reporting is as accurate as it could be. At the end of the day a lot of the employees try to make sure they account for the entire workday and they screw that up a lot."

"How do you know?" asked Howard.

"Pam, in payroll, always complains that the payroll records never reconcile with the shop floor records."

"Yeah, I hear her bitching about that all the time," agreed Scott.

Jim continued, "The machine shop's another story. We do detailed labor reporting by individual job, but it's always frustrated me how the same part can have such large variances."

"What do you mean?" asked Fred.

"With Mary's help, I've charted the actual costs for a single part we run about once a week. Over the last three months, the labor component has ranged from eight dollars per piece to over twenty dollars."

"Really?" said Charles. "What's going on?"

Jim responded, "The part has a standard labor cost of fourteen dollars, so on average we're OK. But I don't know what the part really costs."

Mike interrupted, "Or should cost. That's the most important factor."

"Yeah, I know," acknowledged Jim. "We also measure individual productivity but haven't been able to improve it very much."

"How about your area Charles?" asked Mike.

"My guys spend so much time on labor standards, it drives me crazy. We could save a lot of money if we worked on cost reduction projects rather than take precious time and highly compensated engineers away from their main objectives."

"But don't we need standards to schedule the shop?" asked Jim. "I'd be nervous if we stopped collecting the information for labor standards."

"Before I respond, let me ask a few more questions. How do we account for payroll taxes and all the other benefits?"

"We charge payroll taxes and benefits to overhead," said Scott.

"I was afraid of that," said Mike shaking his head in disbelief. "That's what they did at another company I worked for and I never understood it."

"What's wrong with it?" asked Scott.

"Think about it. If any expense varies directly with direct labor dollars, it's the payroll taxes and benefits associated with those dollars."

"So what do you suggest?"

"There isn't any advantage to charging each individual benefit expense to the specific person or department. It's muda. I suggest all payroll taxes and benefits be grouped and provided for on an overall percentage basis, not only through manufacturing, but throughout the company."

"You mean we just have a set percentage of labor as an overall benefits charge?" asked Mary.

"Exactly."

"Where do we book the difference between the actual costs and the amount charged out?"

"Wherever you want. For convenience sake, we kept the difference on the Balance Sheet and reconciled it semi-annually. It was never much."

Fred joined the discussion. "I agree. I never really liked the way we did it, but nobody ever questioned the status quo. That's a simple change we can make before the start of the new year."

"All of the department heads will appreciate it," said Mike. "They have no control over these expenses because they're either legal mandates or the result of company policy. Now they'll just budget a set percentage of wages and not worry about wild fluctuations due to timing issues or different mixes of employees."

"How about my question earlier, Mike?" asked Scott.

"What was that?"

"You were explaining that benefits expense shouldn't be included in manufacturing overhead."

"Thanks for bringing that up again. If you insist on charging direct labor to individual manufacturing departments, then to be consistent, benefits should follow the labor charges. It makes no sense to flow benefits to an overhead account and then allocate them back to individual products as part of a large overhead pool. It's stupid."

"I like that," said Scott, "that'll save me a lot of work."

"Me, too," said Mary.

"That's just the first step."

"Really?"

"I don't want to jump ahead, but if we stop tracking labor by manufacturing department, you'd be able to consolidate most of the departments."

"That would really be a time saver," agreed Mary.

"At my last company, we went from seventeen manufacturing departments to only four, and the accounting department loved it. Think of all the work it saves in forecasting, budgeting, month end entries, and reclasses."

"Sounds even better," said Scott.

"OK then, let's get back to my overall question."

"What's that?" asked Fred.

"The accuracy of labor standards?" said Mike. "Based on what we've heard so far, how accurate do you think the labor standards are at the discrete product level?"

Everyone thought about the question but no one volunteered an answer, so Mike picked on Mary.

"What do you think, Mary? You're dealing with the numbers every day."

"I was hoping you'd forget that question. The answer's different for each product family depending on the number of operations, the variability of lot sizes, and the frequency of product changes."

"Don't get too technical on me."

"If we're within twenty-five percent of actual labor costs, we're lucky," said Mary in a hushed tone.

"I can't believe you're saying that," said Scott. "You work so hard to keep the cost system accurate. A twenty-five percent error rate is mind boggling."

"You think I'm happy about it? I'm just being honest based on the data Mike's asked us to analyze."

"So you're saying if labor's ten dollars, it could be anywhere from seven-fifty to twelve-fifty?" asked Mike.

"That's right, but it's only a guess. What do you think, Charles? You're staff's constantly in the plant verifying the standards."

"I don't know. It's difficult keeping up with the changes. Besides, we see the labor variances and sometimes they're pretty significant."

"Do you analyze them by product?" asked Howard.

"That's too hard."

Howard pressed the issue, "Why?"

"In the assembly areas, we report by department, so the variances can't be traced to a specific product. In the machining centers, we track everything by job, but any given part can have wild swings in actual run rates due to the operator, set-up procedures, number of pieces in the batch, tooling problems, material, etc. You heard what Jim said earlier about part costs. As much as I hate to admit it, I think you're right Mary."

Mike couldn't help but smile. "So we go to great lengths to try and report labor accurately to the discrete product, but deep down you know it's virtually impossible to get it right."

"I guess you're right," said Charles. "It's like designing a part with dimensional tolerances to the thousandths for a process that can only be controlled to quarter-inch increments. Yet we keep spending more and more resources to do the impossible."

"Great analogy! In a Lean environment, it becomes even harder to track labor to discrete products."

"Why?" asked Howard.

"Jeez, Howard, is that all you ever say," needled Jim.

"Excuuuuse me for wanting to understand this."

"Cut it out, guys," said Mike. "The only way to achieve continuous flow is to have a workforce that's extremely flexible. That requires extensive cross-training so the workforce can move from operation to operation in sync with demand and product mix fluctuations. If it's difficult to accurately track labor now, it'll become impossible in a Lean shop."

"That makes sense," said Howard.

"In addition, with continuous improvement teams, work methods constantly change, making it even more difficult to track labor."

"If the workforce moves from department to department, what happens with our labor grade system?" asked Jim.

"In a Lean plant, employees have a wide range of skills and you promote team over individual achievements. The number of labor grade classifications has to be drastically reduced."

"HR will have a fit over that."

"They had better not. I've seen plants go from more than fifty labor classes to only a handful. Pay practices also have to be redesigned."

"How so?" wondered Jim.

"We implemented pay-for-skills programs throughout the plant. You couldn't walk through the place without seeing charts indicating crosstraining competency by employee. The transition's a lot of work and HR plays a critical role."

"I'll bet," said Jim.

"One more thing. We'll depend on the shop floor

workforce to come up with productivity improvement ideas during the continuous improvement efforts."

"Now I'm worried," said Jim in a very serious tone. "We've had all sorts of suggestion programs and none of them ever did squat for us. Either we didn't get enough quality suggestions, or we were swamped and couldn't evaluate them, let alone implement them. How's this gonna be any different?"

"For starters, it's not a suggestion system. The teams will receive training in Lean techniques and then it'll be their responsibility to come up with the ideas and implement them. A good idea without implementation is a dream."

"But won't they just be working themselves out of a job?"

"Now you've gotten to the core of the issue. You'd make a great straight man for explaining Lean."

Jim smiled and looked around the room for approval. Mary crumpled up some paper and threw it at him.

"What'd you do that for?"

"Because you're so full of yourself."

Mike laughed and continued with his explanation.

"The philosophy of Lean is the people closest to the work have the most knowledge, and if allowed to contribute... no, I mean if they're encouraged to lead the improvement effort, they'll provide innovative solutions. But, they're also very concerned about their own well-being, and industry has unfortunately demonstrated that the 'thank you' for a job well-done is often the elimination of the position."

"You've got that right," said Jim. "They're not fools."

"That's why we'll have to provide a 'No Layoff Pledge' before we undertake any Lean initiatives on the shop floor."

"I can't imagine any company doing that. It'd be

suicide," said Tom.

Everyone nodded in agreement with Tom.

"You can't be serious," said Fred.

"Hold on a second. Before you jump to conclusions, let me explain the pledge."

"Go ahead," said Fred.

"The company has to promise not to lay off any employee as a result of productivity improvements from Lean initiatives. The company also has to make it very clear that they still have a business to run and, in the event the level of business declines, layoffs may still occur."

"Aren't you just playing with words?" asked Fred.

"No," said Mike emphatically. "If business declines, layoffs would most likely occur anyway. But by implementing Lean, we're improving everyone's job security because we'll be much more competitive. Lead-times will be shorter, costs will be reduced, etc. And as productivity increases, additional capacity is created so we can attract new business without adding headcount, thereby increasing everyone's job security."

"That makes a lot of sense. Sounds like another win/win situation, as long as the company holds up its end of the bargain," commented Jim. "It'll also make my job easier if the employees don't hold back anymore."

"They won't if we honor our commitment," agreed Mike.

"I guess Lean taps into their minds, not just their arms and legs."

"Precisely, and everyone's sense of worth skyrockets. A no layoff pledge also makes sense since we'll be spending a lot of time and effort training folks in Lean techniques. Our employees become one of the company's most powerful strategic weapons."

"I'm not sure I understand," said Howard. "If you can still lay off people, what's the difference?"

"If sales stay constant and we have excess labor due to productivity improvements from Lean, we won't lay anyone off," responded Mike. "We may move them to other areas though. That's the message that has to be repeated over and over. If the company ever violates this promise, the Lean journey's over."

"I get it now," said Howard.

"Good, let's get back to the issue of accounting for labor costs."

Christy, who had been quiet up to this point, chimed in.

"It seems obvious now, Mike."

"So enlighten us."

"I'll try," said Christy as she confidently looked at the notes she had been taking. "We agreed the labor standards are not very accurate."

Everyone nodded in agreement.

"Mary demonstrated that labor didn't fluctuate within fairly wide volume bands. Mike explained that keeping up with changes would become more and more difficult. And finally, we need to institute a no layoff policy."

Christy paused to see if everyone was following her. She saw Mike's smile and knew she was on the right track. "Under these circumstances, plant labor is as fixed an expense as anywhere else in the business."

"Given the assumptions, I have to agree," said Fred.

Christy was picking up momentum now. "And, from a total cost point of view, plant labor is less than a lot of our other expenses, particularly S, G & A, which we never assign to individual products. So I don't think we'll lose much by not tracking labor costs at the detailed item level."

"You nailed it," said Mike with a huge grin.

"But what do the folks do when we have a slow month?" asked Howard.

"We'll use the time as an opportunity to work on

improvement projects," responded Mike.

"I don't understand." said Charles. "It makes sense in theory, but how will we schedule the plant? How will we know our product costs? My industrial engineers will think I've gone crazy, not to mention they'll be worried about their jobs."

"I'm not suggesting we immediately stop all existing routines. We still have a business to run, and until we develop new procedures, we shouldn't change a thing."

"Now I'm really confused. After all of this, you're saying we shouldn't change."

"No. No. I'm not saying that. The transition will take years and we have to take it one step at a time. I just want to make sure you understand where we're headed so we can make good decisions along the way."

"I see. But I still don't know how we can schedule the place."

"We'll use different metrics, that's all."

"Like what?" pressed Charles.

"We've been here a long time. I wasn't planning to get into this. What do you all think?"

"We've gone this far, we might as well continue," said Fred.

"Yeah, I agree," said Mary.

"How about the rest of you?"

They all nodded in agreement.

"OK then. As we develop flow techniques, we'll produce product to the drumbeat of the customer."

"And what exactly does that mean?" asked Christy.

"Production will be driven by customer orders, not by a forecast. We'll use a technique called Takt Time to properly staff the production cells. And critical data will be collected on the shop floor in real time so our costs will be more accurate then ever."

"How about the machine shop?" asked Jim.

"We'll use a measurement called OEE, or Operational Equipment Effectiveness."

"Now that's a mouthful," said Charles.

"Instead of the current metrics, such as labor productivity, we'll measure the process. After all, labor productivity is dependent on the processes we provide the employees, from the maintenance of the machines, to the location of the tool room, to material handling techniques, to scheduling. The focus will move from monitoring the person to monitoring the process."

"The operators will like that," noted Jim. "They're always complaining about material availability."

"There are a lot of other metrics we'll use. We won't be operating blind. The major difference is the data will be collected on the plant floor and visually displayed so everyone will know how the plant's doing."

"That'll be cool," said Christy.

"It really is, because the metrics point out areas that need improvement, which in turn are attacked by the continuous improvement teams. It's a closed loop system that feeds upon itself and brings the entire company to the next level. And along the way all the muda is eliminated."

"Mike, you're making it sound too easy," said Charles.

"I don't want you to think it's easy. If it were, everyone would be doing it. The difficulty's not in the intellect required, it's in the commitment, the passion, the willingness to change, the willingness to push the envelope, and the perseverance to stay the course for years and years."

"I guess so," said Charles.

"Let me give you an example. Your engineers have nice offices on the second floor, right?"

"So?"

"When there's a problem on the production floor, they have to be paged, right?"

"That's right."

"In a Lean environment there's no time for that, it's all muda."

"What do you mean?"

"In a Lean facility, everyone's located on the production floor. When there's a problem, the engineers are there to correct the situation. They're part of the floor team, not executives who have to be summoned.

"That's a different approach for sure."

"Most Lean plants have Andon lights that flash when there's a problem. They're very hard to see from an office in the back of the second floor. These are the cultural changes that make a Lean transformation so difficult."

"I see what you mean. It's a good example."

"It's not just an example. We need to do that."

"You mean you really need my guys on the plant floor?"

"Absolutely"

"My guys will go nuts over that. They treasure their offices. It's a right of passage to move from a cubicle to an office, and especially an office with a window. You expect them to give it all up? Isn't that going a little too far?"

"Not if we want to be World Class. Not if they want job security. Not if they want to stay competitive. Not if they expect to work in a North American manufacturing plant ten years from now, because most companies will be practicing Lean or they'll be out of business. It's the people issues that make the Lean transition tough, and it's your job to lead by example."

"Charles, cheer up, we'll find a nice spot for you," bellowed Jim with a huge grin. "I love it."

Charles just slouched in his chair and didn't offer a response.

Mike continued, "Charles, we spoke earlier about how an individual part can have an actual labor cost of anywhere from eight to twenty dollars and it's OK, because on average, the cost equals the accounting standard of fourteen dollars. In a Lean environment that's unacceptable. Your engineers, working with the operators, would be required to standardize the process to consistently produce the part for eight dollars, and then develop a game plan to continuously lower costs. A flow environment would not function with such variability."

"And I thought your area was the only one getting picked on, Fred. Now I'm starting to squirm."

Fred responded, "I see the logic in it. Accounting deals in materiality and averages, Lean gets to the raw data to drive improvement."

Mary elbowed Christy and whispered, "Fred's getting on board." Christy smiled back.

"How about my question, Mike? You still haven't answered it. How can we have more accurate costs by tracking fewer items?" asked Tom.

"I'll answer it. But I've got to warn you, it's pretty involved."

"There's no turning back now," said Christy.

"Material's about sixty-five percent of product costs, and I'm sure what we track is very accurate. But there are components of material costs that we ignore..."

"Like what?" interrupted Jim.

"Inbound freight, inventory allowances, scrap, material usage variances, purchase price variances, and hardware."

"We don't ignore them," said Mary defensively.

"But you don't trace them to discrete products."

"It's too difficult."

"So they're included in overhead or expensed directly to the Income Statement. Together they total about seven percent of total product costs, or ten percent of material costs."

"I never thought about it that way," said Scott.

"Most folks don't. So for starters, material, at best,

is only about ninety percent accurate at the discrete product level due to the missing items. Does everyone agree?" Mike asked.

Everyone nodded in agreement. Mike went to the white board and wrote down – Material – 90% accurate. He continued with his explanation.

"We agreed labor's about seventy-five percent accurate. It's really worse than that because payroll taxes and benefits are included in overhead, and therefore direct labor's understated. Also, labor variances of about four percent are not assigned to discrete product costs. I'd bet labor's about sixty percent accurate. Do you agree?"

"It's less accurate than I originally thought. You're probably in the ballpark," said Mary.

"Good." Mike wrote down – Labor – 60%.

"That leaves overhead. I've never seen a methodology to determine its validity."

"Neither have I," said Fred.

"We couldn't determine the accuracy of overhead at the discrete product level if our lives depended on it. Let's say overhead is twenty-five to fifty percent accurate. Will you accept that?"

Once Mary nodded in agreement, they all went along.

Mike wrote down – Overhead – 25%-50%. He made some calculations and summarized them for everyone.

"So then, based on these numbers, overall product costs are seventy-three to seventy-eight percent accurate."

"I can't argue that," said Mary.

"In Lean, we'd get the material component as accurate as possible and rely on it for most decisions."

"What do you mean?" asked Howard.

"If I got material ninety-five to ninety-eight percent accurate by properly including all the components, wouldn't that be good enough?"

"You wouldn't include labor or overhead?"

"Why should I? We already said total material is about seventy-two percent of product costs. If I can raise the accuracy of the material component, that's as far as I'd go at the discrete product level. The accuracy wouldn't be significantly different from what's currently reported."

"Boy, would that save a lot of work," said Mary.

"It sure does. In the meantime, by virtue of Lean methods, obsolescence, scrap, and labor variances would be reduced significantly. Decision making would be as good, if not better, with a material only costing system."

"So my engineers would refocus their efforts to process improvements," said Charles.

"Absolutely. And the same applies for Mary's staff. I've gone through the calculations to show that accuracy's really not sacrificed in Lean. The focus is getting everyone involved in improvement activities instead of traditional monitoring efforts."

"I understand," said Tom. "You also avoid making poor decisions because of bad information."

Everyone nodded in agreement.

"I believe that leaves just one question unanswered. Fred wanted to know why other companies haven't adopted this approach."

"I've been thinking about that all along," said Fred.

"You probably know the answer by now."

"I think so. First of all, changing our methodology would require a significant adjustment in our thinking, from pricing formulas, to target costs in product development, to profitability analyses. A lot of education would be required to transition to a material only cost system, and most companies see no reason to make such a dramatic change."

"That's right, it's a lot of hard work."

Fred continued. "Second, new routines would have

to be developed to properly account for inventory. With a material only cost system we'd be excluding labor and overhead from product costs, but we'd still have to properly value inventory for GAAP and tax reporting. Accounting usually doesn't have time to change all of the reporting routines."

"Right again, you're on a roll."

"You the man," yelled out Jim.

"Finally, there's no impetus to change accounting practices unless you're implementing Lean. And from what I understand, there aren't very many companies doing it."

"You're right. And even the companies implementing Lean have a tendency to just focus on the manufacturing area. Sooner or later they run into a brick wall because the other departments don't understand what's going on. Then the admin areas have to catch up, and it slows down the entire journey."

"That's why you're putting us through this hell now?" joked Christy.

"Yep. At Lean Alliance meetings, I hear complaint after complaint about accounting's unwillingness to embrace Lean techniques. It drives a wedge between accounting and manufacturing. It takes a lot more time up front to involve everyone, but it leads to the best results."

"Makes a lot of sense," said Jim.

"I'd like to add one more item to your list, Fred."

"Be my guest."

"It's difficult to envision tangible benefits by implementing Lean in the office area. That's why everyone focuses on the factory floor–that's where all the big gains will be achieved, or so they think. Getting all the silos working together from the beginning will maximize the benefits and speed up the journey."

"Makes sense," said Fred.

"Trust me, I've implemented Lean both ways, and

it's a bitch doing it alone."

"But what did you mean by the comment 'or so they think'?"

"I didn't want to get into that now, but as long as you asked..."

"C'mon, boss, you weren't going to skip anything. Don't BS us."

"I was. I'll explain what I meant and then let's move on. We don't have time to get into it now."

"It's a deal, boss."

"Tangible benefits are readily visible on the production floor and can be achieved in months, or even days. It's visible and can generate excitement. But my background's finance and I know the gains on the production floor, while significant, can be dwarfed by product development if they jumped on the Lean bandwagon. Imagine the bottom-line impact of getting new products to market in half the time with less start up problems. I've said fifty to seventy-five percent of everything we do in manufacturing is waste. Well, the same holds true for the product development process. But it's the toughest nut to crack."

"So when do we focus on that?" asked Christy.

"We have enough on our plates now. Hopefully, next year."

"Mike, I'm beginning to understand the implications of Lean," said Fred. "I was as big a skeptic as there was, but it's beginning to come together."

"I'm really glad to hear that. I hope you all feel that way."

Everyone nodded.

Fred continued. "I have a better understanding about what needs to be done, but the specifics still aren't clear."

"I know what you mean," said Mary. "I still have a lot of questions."

"Like what?" asked Mike.

Fred responded. "For instance, how do you treat direct labor on the Income Statement, in what order are the changes made, and over what time period? What are the implications for the IT area, etc.? Understanding where we want to go and getting there are two different things. We'll need help with the transition."

"We'll meet separately to discuss a transition plan and the detailed steps."

"That'd be great."

"How about me, what do I tell my guys about labor standards?"

"One step at a time, Charles."

"How about IT, Mike?" asked Christy.

"You'll have to support all the changes. I'm afraid you'll have to undo a lot of the routines you spent so much time building."

"That's what it sounds like. I'm still not sure what role our MRP system plays in a Lean environment. Also, how do I finish my current projects and work on the Lean transformation?"

"How about the General Ledger, Mike?" asked Tom. "How will we collect product costs on the shop floor and feed them to the accounting system? How will we value work in process inventory?"

Howard joined the question brigade. "Mike, how will sales and marketing use the cost system to make pricing decisions if all the standards change? How will we develop target costs for product development?"

"OK already. The questions require separate discussions, but the answers are pretty straightforward."

Fred responded. "It sounds like we need a plan for the functional areas."

"You're right. I'll meet with each department separately. I'll set some meetings up over the next few months. It's a long journey; we can't do everything at once. I need to get some things going on the manufacturing floor first."

The meeting adjourned. As Fred left the room he pulled Mike aside.

"I wanted to let you know I contacted your references."

"I hope they weren't too hard on me."

"On the contrary, they spoke highly of you. They made it clear you were instrumental in improving the performance of their companies. Maybe you're not such a jerk after all."

"I haven't exactly been the easiest person to put up with."

"I'll second that. We've got to learn to work together."

"I'm trying. I don't mean to be so aggressive, I just can't help it. I can't stand seeing all the waste. We can make tremendous improvements but I need your help."

"You have my support. I retire in three years, so I have no time to lose if I'm going to be part of a success story."

"You will be. And we'll need all of the three years."

"Really."

"Afraid so. We've only really discussed cost accounting. We need to spend time on a transition plan for all of Lean Accounting, including financial statements, target costing, product family statements, and inventory valuation. There's a lot more to this than cost systems."

"I'm learning that. Let me know when you want to get together to discuss the next steps."

"It'd be best if we discussed a rough timetable first. Let's do that soon."

"OK, I'll set something up. Who should I bring?"

"Tom and Mary."

"I'm looking forward to it."

"By the way, Mike, I heard you lost some people

in Boston. What happened?"

"I'll kill Jack. What did the son-of-a-gun tell you?"

"Nothing, he wanted me to ask you. What happened?"

"I was trying to rally the troops and thought it'd be a good idea to take the folks from the plant to a Red Sox game. I didn't realize some of them had never been out of Vermont before and were more interested in doing other things in the big city, like visiting the notorious combat zone. When the game was over, we were missing three employees. All weekend I worried that nothing happened to them. They finally showed up at work on Monday and we all had a good laugh."

"I bet you never did that again."

"The plant had something to talk about for weeks. It was great except I was scared shitless until they showed up."

Mike headed back to his office. I hope I haven't created a monster now, he thought. If Fred gets too aggressive he could lose control of the financial reports. He'd have to guard against that.

Meanwhile Scott, Mary, Tom, and Howard gathered in Tom's office. Mary spoke first. "I guess we don't have to worry about Fred digging in his heels over Lean anymore."

"We sure don't," said Tom. "I wonder what happened?"

Howard responded, "We'll probably never find out. As long as we move ahead it's fine with me. I'm ready for some changes."

They nodded in agreement and left for their offices.

23 The Transition Plan

"Fred's starting to worry me now," said Tom as he walked down the corridor with Scott to meet Mike and discuss the steps required to transition from a full absorption cost system to a material only cost system.

"I know. It was so frustrating to watch him dig in his heels over every comment Mike made. But now I'm worried he's hell bent on implementing this stuff. It'll get all screwed up if we're not careful."

"I hope Mike doesn't let him run wild with the changes."

"I doubt it. He doesn't want a mess either."

"It's about time you guys showed up," said Fred as Tom and Scott walked into the conference room.

"Sorry about that. We were finishing up a conference call," responded Tom as he took a seat in the back of the room.

"Fred, how about if I explain how we transitioned cost systems at my previous companies and then we can discuss what's relevant here?" asked Mike.

"That's fine."

"First of all, the transition to Lean Accounting doesn't happen over night. I've gone to a material only cost system twice, and each time it took three years."

"Three years!" gasped Fred. "That's incredible! Why so long?"

"It's a methodical process, or at least it was for us.

The first thing we did was remove overhead costs from the cost standards. In concept it's pretty easy, but in practice it's a lot of work, especially for Mary's group."

"I've been thinking about that, and I have some ideas," said Mary.

"Let me go through what we did, and if you can improve on it, super."

"Go ahead."

"First we examined our manufacturing costs and determined which would be classified as fixed costs. If you remember the example I gave you about electricity, you know it's not that easy."

"That's for sure," said Scott.

"Any expense that was virtually unaffected by volume fluctuations during the prior twelve-month period was included in a new cost center called Manufacturing Fixed Costs. We reversed all the allocation schemes used to assign these costs to the other cost centers."

"That doesn't sound too bad," said Mary.

"It wasn't. Included in the new cost center were depreciation, utilities, supplies, travel, manufacturing supervision, etc. So instead of distributing depreciation expense to ten or twenty cost centers, we charged the entire expense to the Manufacturing Fixed Cost department."

"I like it," said Mary. "What else?"

"If a cost component previously classified as material was reclassified as a fixed cost, such as electricity, then the bills of material were adjusted."

"What happened at month-end?" asked Howard.

"We charged all fixed costs directly to the Income Statement."

"You had to," said Mary.

"You're right. It was necessary because the cost components moved to the Fixed Cost department were no longer included in the standard cost of the product. The traditional standard cost of sales entry would understate the actual cost of sales."

Mary commented, "I assumed that would be the process. I've been trying to figure out how long it would take to redo all the rates."

"What do you think?"

"We could probably do it in a couple of months."

"Don't rush it. You'll lose control of the financials if you're not careful. We don't want to do anything foolish."

"I'm glad to hear that," said Tom. "Wouldn't it be much easier to make the financial changes at year-end so the entire fiscal year's operating under the same cost system?"

"I'm for that," said Howard. "It's hard enough reporting year-to-year financial comparisons in a consistent fashion, I'd hate to compound the problem by having different cost systems during the year."

"You're right," said Mike. "That's why the conversion takes so long. The window of opportunity is very small each year. And we're only talking about the first step in the process, accounting for fixed manufacturing costs. The second step, eliminating direct labor, usually follows in the next fiscal year."

"So we either get it done in the next couple of months or we'll have to wait a year?" asked Fred.

"That's right. That's a decision you'll have to make."

"We don't have much time then," said Fred shaking his head in disgust.

"That's why I wanted to have these meetings."

"Are you sure we can't do it mid-year?"

"I don't know. I've never done it and I don't want to start now. If you can recalculate everything prior to year-end, great, but it's your choice. Let's go over the other steps before you make any decisions. Once the calculations are completed, you'll store the new standard costs in a separate file, perhaps the "Going To" cost file, if you aren't using it already. At the beginning of the new fiscal year we'd begin using the *Going To* file."

"That's not a problem, but what about the Balance Sheet?" asked Mary.

"What do you think?"

"At the end of this year, I'll run the perpetual inventory based on the *Current* standard costs as well as the *Going To* standard costs."

"And then what?"

"Obviously the inventory will be much lower for the *Going To* inventory valuation since the standard costs won't contain the fixed manufacturing components."

"Bingo."

"What do I do with the difference?"

"Let me answer that," said Fred.

"Go ahead," said Mike, pleased Fred was an active participant this time.

"The difference in the two inventory valuations represents the amount of fixed costs removed, or extracted, from the item-by-item inventory records. It still has to be reported as inventory. What do you call it?"

"I've always categorized the extracted inventory costs as a separate line item on the Balance Sheet entitled "Fixed Costs in Inventory" right below the Inventory at Standard account."

"That makes sense," said Mary. "We're just dividing the inventory balance into two components; the first is the standard cost containing labor, material, and other variable costs, and the second contains all the fixed costs in a lump sum."

"You got it. The concept isn't hard—it's the execution that takes time."

Christy added, "There's a lot of data to process, but if Mary and I work together, we can develop some programs that'll simplify the process."

"I'm sure you can, but there are other nuances that'll cause problems."

"Like what?" asked Christy.

"I can think of a couple right off the bat," said Mary. "Where we have a lot of work in process, or semi-finished inventory, it won't be so easy."

"Yeah, you're right, that'll be a problem," said Tom.

"It sure will," responded Mary. "Depending where the pay points are, and the length of time in process, we'll have some inventory valuation issues at year-end."

"Another problem is our transfer pricing policy," said Fred. "We've set procedures for charging our sister companies when we ship product from one Tricor legal entity to another. It's a sticky issue for our international subsidiaries because taxes and duty are driven by the transfer price."

"You're right," said Tom. "We've spent a lot of time and money working with our auditors to defend our international pricing agreements with the local authorities. We have precedents we don't want to jeopardize. If we're not careful, the changes could cost the company a lot of money in unnecessary taxes."

"I agree," said Mike. "The inventory valuation problem created by work in process at year-end is minor and can be estimated. However, complying with the existing transfer price policy is an issue."

"What did you do?" asked Fred.

"During my first Lean transformation, I was concerned about pricing integrity so we developed automated routines to calculate the fixed cost associated with each item. Rather than bury the fixed costs in the standard cost, we calculated it separately for each item based on labor dollars. We kept the data in a separate file and at month-end consolidated the fixed costs into one entry. If we needed the full cost of an item, it was readily available."

"That hardly sounds like a Lean approach," Christy commented with a grin. "You really didn't change anything."

"You're right, we cheated. We were scared to abandon assigning all costs to individual items, so we just hid them in another file. No one was doing Lean Accounting and we were making up the rules as we went, so we created more work for ourselves."

"So you created muda," pointed out Fred.

"Sure did. In my second transformation we abandoned the calculation of fixed costs by item and instead rewrote our transfer pricing policies based only on variable costs. We just changed the pricing formulas to arrive at the same pricing that was in place prior to the cost system changes. After all, the economics of the situation hadn't changed. We saved a lot of time and systems effort."

"I like that better," said Christy. It'll save my IT department a lot of time."

It was Tom's turn to ask some questions. "So what else?"

"You're going to have a lot more work."

"Like I don't have enough already. Why?"

"Everyone likes to compare financial statements on a comparative basis with prior-year activity."

"Ain't that the truth."

"Before the new year started, we restated the prior year as if the new cost system had been in place. It provides a greater level of comfort for everyone.

"Then the budget has to be prepared in a similar fashion, doesn't it?" asked Fred.

"It sure does. That's where all the effort is, restating everything so everyone understands it. That's when you really learn what it's all about."

Fred leaned back in his chair and started to rub his forehead. "It's gonna be a lot of work."

"There's one more thing," said Mike. "A lot of the

key performance indicators will change. Let me give you a few examples."

"That would help," said Scott.

"Monthly scrap expense will be lower since the new standard costs of scrapped parts will be less. Everyone will think scrap's gone down when nothing's really changed. Likewise, individual product margins, warranty, and any other measure involving product costs will be affected."

"You're starting to overwhelm me," said Mary.

"The technical side of the financial transition is relatively easy. It's the communication of the new reporting system and its impact on decision making that's the tough part."

"I guess that responsibility would fall on my shoulders," said Fred.

"You bet. You'll have to conduct educational sessions throughout the company. It's critical. No matter how much I explained it, the non-financial folks at my previous companies had trouble with it. It takes time to get used to the new metrics."

"Fortunately, I have a very good relationship with Randy and Steve. They'll understand."

"It won't be that easy, Fred, I guarantee it."

"I think you neglected one issue, Mike," commented Scott. "How are Fixed Manufacturing Costs reported on the monthly Income statement?"

"Glad you brought it up. The easiest way is to charge the monthly Fixed Costs directly to the Income Statement. As long as inventory turns don't change, it's the correct entry."

"But they will change," said Mary. "We've already proved that."

"When that happens we'll need to recalculate the amount of Fixed Costs on the Balance Sheet at month-end. The correct amount can be determined by a number of methods."

"I hope it's easy," said Scott.

"It is. I've always calculated the month-end balance by dividing full year estimated fixed costs by the most recent twelve-month inventory turns. It approximates the proportion of full year fixed costs that should be in inventory at month-end."

"Do we have to do it monthly?" wondered Mary.

"No. Depending on the dynamics of the business, the calculation can be made monthly or quarterly. When I was with a seasonal business, inventory swings were significant, so we did it monthly. With my other company, quarterly adjustments were sufficient."

"So what about the Income Statement?" asked Scott.

"When the balance in the Fixed Cost in Inventory account has to be adjusted, the correcting amounts are flowed through the Income Statement via a Fixed Cost (to)/from inventory account."

Scott responded, "I guess we won't really know what's involved until we try it. We ought to do it monthly so we don't have any surprises at the end of the quarter."

"You bet," said Fred. "I'm not going to wait until the end of the quarter to see what impact there'll be."

"That's what I'd recommend. You'll work out the kinks when you try to budget it. So what do you think, Fred, still want to implement the changes now?"

"If we're going to do it, I don't want to wait another year. I'm confident the people in this room can get it done. What do you think?"

"That's a dangerous question. I always want to go for it."

"Yeah, why did I even ask."

"I'm worried, it's close to year-end and you have a lot on your plate. It's your decision. I'll help any way I can."

"One more thing. I assume the same process applies for removing labor from the cost system."

"You got it. That usually follows in the next fiscal year. That's what I've always done. Once labor was removed from the standards, we charged it directly to the Income Statement as a line item entitled Processing Costs. There's also a corresponding account on the Balance Sheet entitled Processing Costs in Inventory, which is also adjusted monthly or quarterly, based on inventory turns."

"Makes sense."

"So now can you understand how this can take two to three years to implement."

"I sure do," said Fred. "It'll be awhile before we get to a material only cost system."

"The cost system changes don't end with the adoption of a material only cost system."

"Why not?" asked Mary.

"Think about it for a second. What's the end game?"

"I'm not sure I understand."

"As a company implements Lean, they get better and better at managing inventory. Eventually they begin to produce to the exact pull of the customer with very little inventory. Material flows so fast that inventory spins instead of turns. Imagine if we had fifty-two inventory spins a year."

"That's hard to imagine. Can it really be done?" asked Scott.

"Sure. And then most of the accounting entries we just discussed would be muda. Rather then concerning ourselves with inventory changes, we'd just charge all production expenses immediately to cost of sales. The inventory level would be fixed at one week and any differences would be ignored because they'd be immaterial."

"Does it ever end?" asked Fred.

"There are always improvements, that's why Lean's

a journey. If you decide to wait on the cost system changes, there'll be a lot of other things to work on."

"Like what," asked Tom.

"You can all participate in shop floor projects, conduct 5S activities in accounting, assist with value stream mapping and process improvement efforts in the admin areas, and change the payment system to accommodate electronic kanbans for starters."

"Let me think about it," said Fred. "I want to discuss it with everybody and assess the risk of moving forward."

As the group got up to leave, Fred motioned to his staff to remain in the room. Mike left and Fred addressed the group.

"I know I've been defensive about Mike's suggestions, but after hearing him out I've come to appreciate the merits of Lean Accounting. I'm willing to do whatever it takes to start the process immediately. I'd like each of you to give me your thoughts by tomorrow afternoon."

Fred then got up and left the room with everyone trailing behind him. Mary, Christy, and Tom discussed Fred's comments in the privacy of Christy's office. Christy went first.

"Wow, do you believe Fred wants to go for it? What a turn around."

Tom commented, "He certainly doesn't feel threatened by Mike anymore. I hope he's not being too aggressive. What's your take on it Mary?"

"I think we can do it. Besides, if this is the future of accounting at manufacturing companies, then it's in our best interests to bite the bullet now. It's just so frustrating to find out how useless my work's been to the manufacturing folks."

"It's a real bummer," said Christy.

"It sure is. If this provides everyone with better information, then I'm ready to do whatever's necessary. I don't want to continue to waste my time."

"Me neither. I'll do whatever it takes," said Tom. Christy nodded in agreement.

Meanwhile Scott and Howard were discussing the meeting in Howard's office.

"What do you think?" asked Scott. "These changes will drive you crazy preparing the budget."

"Maybe not. We've already provided the Board with the preliminary budget. Changing the cost system won't change the bottom line, just the presentation."

"Presentation's everything with the Board. If they don't understand the numbers, it'll be a huge problem."

"They see it in summary fashion, so it won't be a big deal. As long as Peter and Fred can explain everything, it'll be OK."

"I hope you're right."

"The biggest problem will be reporting the January numbers. Something's bound to go wrong and our month- end closing for January will be a nightmare."

"There'll be too much going on."

"I'll ask Fred to get an extension on January's reporting schedule. It shouldn't be a problem because it's not a quarterly report."

"Good idea. If it's not a big problem for you, then we should do it. It's going to be a hell of a December."

Fred headed home that evening with a lot on his mind. He was excited about embarking on a major project but didn't want his enthusiasm clouding his judgment. Another talk with Sheila would help him sort out his options.

During dinner Sheila initiated the discussion.

"So why are you in such a good mood?"

"I had a good meeting with Mike today."

"Did he offer to resign?"

"Don't give me a hard time."

"Why not, it's so much fun?"

"He had a lot of good ideas. Now I need to decide if we go full speed ahead."

"Is it all or nothing?"

"Not really. But the major stuff has to happen at year-end and I'd really like to get going."

"So what's stopping you?"

"If I go ahead with it, I'll be totally consumed for the next few months."

"What else is new at year-end?"

"It'll be even worse. Don't expect to see much of me."

"Just like the good old days. Are you sure you want to do this?"

"If I wait a year, I'll be retired before we're operational with Lean."

"I thought you wanted to coast until retirement."

"Don't rub it in. I'm pretty excited about the changes."

"So what's the problem?"

"I can burn out my staff and possibly lose control of the financial statements. When you change everything, you lose comparative benchmarks. It's difficult to detect problems."

"I see."

"I can't leave Peter exposed. He depends on me to provide accurate information. What do you think?"

"Talk to Peter. Your staff's probably excited about the learning experience and will want to proceed, but without Peter's support you can't do it."

"I'll talk to him tomorrow. He's back from his trip and I'm sure he's anxious to know what's going on."

24 Fred's Decision

While driving to the office, Fred kept mulling over the pros and cons of changing the cost system. And the more he thought about it, the easier it seemed to be.

Upon arriving at his office, Fred scheduled a ten o'clock meeting with Peter. Then he called Mike to inform him of his decision.

"Mike, it's Fred."

"What's up?"

"I wanted to let you know I'm going to ask Peter for his approval to implement the cost system changes. I want to make sure I haven't overlooked anything."

"What does your staff think? There's a lot of work that has to be done."

"I'll discuss it with them after I meet with Peter. They'll be OK with the decision. You convinced them."

"What if they're not ready?"

"Then I won't do it. Am I getting too aggressive?"

"You're asking me. You must be kidding."

"Seriously, what do you think?"

"As long as everyone's on board, you'll be OK. But Peter's buy-in is crucial. The changes will affect every area, especially Sales, Marketing, and Product Development. You need to make that clear to Peter."

"I will. I'm planning to work up some examples of the old and new cost system to review with Charles, Randy, and Steve."

"Don't underestimate the amount of education that'll be required. They'll fight you every step of the way if they don't understand it."

"Thanks for the warning. I'll let you know how the meeting with Peter goes."

"Good luck!"

At ten o'clock Fred headed down to Peter's office. Peter was at his desk going through a stack of correspondence that had built up during his three-week trip.

"Welcome back," said Fred. "It looks like you have a lot of catching up to do."

"That's the worst part," Peter said as he pointed to the stack of correspondence. "I don't mind travelling, but I hate coming back to this mess. It'll take me two days to catch up."

"How were the meetings?"

"As expected. Our investors are getting impatient. They want earnings growth and they want it now. All the talk about long-term investing is bullshit. If we don't improve the bottom line, the institutional investors will cash out. And since we're thinly traded, any sell off will pummel our stock."

"I know."

"And the inventory write-down was a real problem. Joe gave me some token support but it was useless."

"He won't be happy until you're outta here. You know that."

"If earnings don't improve next year, he'll get his way. Never mind Joe, how are you and Mike getting along?"

"Much better. I understand what he's trying to accomplish and it makes sense. That's why I came down to see you."

"What do you mean?"

"To implement Lean, many of our accounting practices have to be modified. I'd like to begin immediately, and I'd like your support."

"Why do you need my support?"

"We'll have to change the cost system which means all of the reporting metrics will change—pricing routines, new product cost targets, financial reporting, and just about everything. Everyone's comfort zone about historical margins, mark-ups, and the like will be, I hate to say it, destroyed. They'll resist the change, and without your support I'll have a difficult time convincing everyone."

"Given what you've been through, can you blame them?"

"I guess not."

"Do we really have to do this now, when the Board's breathing down my neck?"

"Implementing Lean's a never-ending process, and I'd just as soon begin now. It'll also help Mike with his improvement initiatives, and we certainly need them."

"Are you sure you can handle it with everything else you've got on your plate?"

"It won't be easy, but it'll get done."

"How about our financial statements, what impact will it have?"

"It won't change our external reporting, just our internal statements."

"Good. Are there any other potential business risks I should be aware of?"

"The financial results for January likely will be late. We expect some minor problems and would like two extra weeks to play it safe."

"That shouldn't be a problem. The monthly results are only for internal purposes. Make sure you clear the changes with our auditing firm."

"I've already scheduled a meeting with the audit partner for tomorrow. There shouldn't be any problems."

"If they sign off on it then go ahead."

"Great. I'll get back to you after the meeting."

Fred left Peter's office pumped up about the impending changes. He could hardly wait until the end of the day to meet with his staff and get their buy in.

At about four o'clock he called everyone into his office.

Mary spoke first. "It'll be hell, but I want to do it. The sooner we start, the sooner we'll reap the rewards. I don't want to change standards mid-year. Besides, it'll be a lot easier after the changes."

"I'm not so sure," said Tom. "Anytime we mess with the systems we always have problems. Mary, you're just thinking about the cost system, but there's a hell of a lot more I have to worry about."

"Like what?" asked Mary.

"The year-end audit, the annual report, SEC filings to name a few. I don't know if we can handle it."

"We'll have the same issues next year."

"Not really, we'll have more time to get our ducks in order."

"C'mon Tom, we'll give you all the support you need," said Howard.

"If we need it, I'll get some help from our accounting firm," said Fred.

"That'll help. Hey, I want to do this as much as all of you; I'm just worried. But if you all think we can do it, I'll give it my best shot."

Howard added, "I've just one request, I'd like to get an extension for January's financial close."

"I've already spoken with Peter about it. How does an additional two weeks sound?"

"That'll be good. It'll give us time to work out the kinks,"

"And I'm sure we'll have some," said Fred. "Mike warned me. But we'll be able to handle them. Does anybody else have any comments?"

"Sounds like a go," said Christy. "I'm all for it."

The Accounting Lean transformation was about to begin.

25 S&OP Meeting—
Three Months Later

It was mid-March and the group gathered for the monthly S&OP meeting. Mike was pushing hard in manufacturing with kanbans, installing new metrics, implementing 5S and set-up reduction events, and installing demand flow techniques in a small pilot cell. He felt good about his progress.

Fred's team, working enormous hours, completed the first phase of the transition to a variable cost system with a few minor problems. They needed every bit of the two extra weeks to complete the January financial reporting package. Fred was ready for the next Lean challenge.

"Mike, please bring everyone up to date on Lean activities," asked Peter.

"Sure," said Mike as he rushed to the front of the room and began to go over each of the initiatives.

"As you know, we started the Lean effort by selecting a number of work centers to 5S. We've completed three areas and plan on doing a work center per month until all key areas are completed. It'll take about two years to complete..."

"Mike, I've been on the road quite a bit the last few months and have no idea what a 5S is," said Steve. "I've heard a lot of jokes about it and some are pretty nasty. Could you explain it?"

"Sure, if nobody minds, I'll go through it again."

"Go ahead," added Randy. "My guys think it's a big joke as well, and I don't know enough to convince them otherwise."

"Their reactions are typical. I was hoping the educational sessions would help, but it takes time and participation to convince everyone. 5S is a process to create a clean, orderly, and efficient workplace."

"What does 5S stand for again?" asked Steve.

"The 5 S's stand for Sort, Straighten, Sweep, Schedule, and Sustain. A 5S event applies these principles to a work center over an intensive three-day period."

"Who's involved?"

"To get the best results, a 5S team includes employees from the target work center plus employees from other areas, including the office, to provide "fresh eyes" to the process. For our first 5S event we included the operators, a supervisor, Mary, a maintenance person, a design engineer from your group, Randy, a manufacturing engineer from Charles's area, and someone from Quality. Mixing people from different areas results in more creative solutions."

"Creative solutions, I thought we're talking about cleaning machines," said Steve shaking his head.

"It's a lot more than just cleaning," said Mike.

Charles joined the discussion. "I agree with Randy. My guys thought it was stupid having the team walk around the plant wearing orange vests. Is that really necessary?"

"They wear the orange vests for a number of reasons."

"Like what?" asked Charles.

"The vests help the team members and the facilitator keep track of each other. They also provide a visual signal to the rest of the plant that an event is underway. We don't want it to be a secret, we want everyone to take notice."

"I guess that makes sense."

"The vests also provide an easy way for the rest of the employees to see who's participating. When they see management, especially Peter, taking part they'll realize we're serious about Lean. Finally, the vests, in perhaps a corny way, foster team spirit. Trust me, it works."

"Boy did my guy take a ribbing from his buddies," said Randy. "They couldn't get over him spending three days cleaning a machine when he had design engineering projects to complete. And did they ever get on him about painting the machine a light crème color."

"Again, that's a typical response. What did the engineer think?"

"He liked the 5S. He just wasn't able to convince the other guys. He wished they had attended the same class so they'd understand it."

"Part of the process is "just in time" education. I'd like to teach the entire company at once, but it doesn't work; they forget everything. As we form project teams, I'll run mini classes. Then it's up to the team to do its best to spread the word. It'll take awhile before most of the employees are convinced, but we have no choice."

"That's fine for you to say," said Steve, "but it's annoying to hear everyone laughing about it, especially when we have our own doubts."

"Why don't you join an event so you can see for yourself what 5S is all about."

"You gotta be kidding. I don't have the time."

"I'm scheduled for the next event, and if I can find time, so can you," said Peter. "We need to demonstrate our commitment to the troops."

"Does that mean you'll be wearing an orange vest?"

"It sure does," responded Peter.

They all looked at each other. Mike glanced toward Peter and smiled. He was looking forward to Peter legitimizing the event.

Randy commented again, "Peter, let me know when you're part of the 5S event. I want to get a picture of you in the vest."

They all had a good laugh.

Peter turned to Fred and asked, "Mary was on the first 5S team, what did she think?"

"I wish she were here to tell you herself, because, to use her words, she was blown away by the event."

"Why?" asked Randy.

"As the accountant on the team, she developed baseline metrics for the work center prior to the event."

"Metrics before you clean an area. I'm lost," said Randy.

"She calculated the space required, the inventory of parts, set-up times, etc. Mike also gave her a new metric to use for the machining centers, OEE, or Operational Equipment Effectiveness. It's the product of Equipment Availability (EA) times Equipment Efficiency (EFF) times Quality (EQ). Mary tracked it for three weeks prior to the event."

"Slow down Fred. What does OEQ mean in English?" asked Randy.

"It's OEE." Fred went to the board to explain. "It's a performance measure for equipment. It's the product of EA, Equipment Availability, times EFF, efficiency, times EQ, Quality. EA is equipment run time as a percentage of scheduled available time. EFF is the equipment's actual run speed versus the theoretical or nameplate speed of the machine. And EQ is the number of good pieces produced compared to the total number of pieces produced. Does that help?"

"Yeah, I think so. I'm trying to keep up with you on this."

Fred continued. "Everyone in accounting was surprised when Mary shared the results. The work center had an OEE of only 40% prior to the event. We were stunned. The usual financial measures would never reveal such poor performance. While the objective of 5S isn't necessarily to improve the OEE, it still improved from 40% to 50% two weeks after the event. And the space required was cut by a third."

The response got Charles's attention. "Why did the OEE improve so much? I thought our manufacturing engineers set some pretty tough standards."

"They do, given the work environment. But if the place is totally disorganized, tools are missing, and material handling is haphazard, production rates are lower than they should be. Mike said set-up times would be reduced as a result of 5S, but no one believed him."

"So was that why the OEE increased?"

"Absolutely. The set-ups improved because wasted motion was eliminated and the operators didn't have to look for their tools. The EA part of the equation increased because the percentage of time devoted to running parts increased. The quality also improved because the operators were more focused."

Steve commented, "Sounds like a spring cleaning to me. We're investing a lot of time cleaning something that'll just become a mess again in a month or two. That's what everyone's talking about."

"That couldn't be farther from the truth," said Mike. "It's a lot more than a spring cleaning."

"You'll have a hard time convincing me," insisted Steve.

"OEE increases because work methods are improved. Cleaning the equipment includes a thorough inspection to identify oil leaks and other problems that are hidden due to workplace clutter. All work carts and tables were cut in half and mounted on wheels to minimize space required and to facilitate movement for daily cleaning."

"I wondered why you did that," said Randy.

"The operators spent thirty minutes a day cleaning up the mess, now it takes only ten minutes. The team designed countermeasures to prevent the mess from occurring in the first place. Shields were built to catch metal chips, channels were created to catch oil, and all unnecessary items were removed, including equipment and tooling that hadn't been used in years. Safety was also improved as new racks were created to eliminate operator bending and reaching. Finally, the equipment was painted a light color to make it easier to see problems."

"I don't understand." said Steve.

"In most plants, heavy machinery is painted a dark color to hide problems. With Lean, we want to highlight problems and fix them immediately before a production line is unexpectedly shut down. You can't hide a problem with white machines."

Fred was anxious to join in again. "What impressed me most were the comments Mary made about her newfound understanding of the process. She learned more in three days about process waste than she could ever learn in a cost accounting text or by looking at cost variances. Variance reporting doesn't reveal the efficiencies an operation could achieve. She's confident throughput in the work center will set records, especially after the team focuses on set–up reductions. And it's happening because people are working smarter, not harder."

"You're right," said Mike. "The accountants at my last company had no idea what the products were until they participated in Lean events. They knew every product by its acronym, such as PRL, MBT, TRN, etc., but they couldn't pick out a product in a lineup if their lives depended on it. They appreciated the opportunity to learn the product line."

"So why aren't all of the other companies doing 5S events?" asked Steve.

"Because it's freakin' hard work," said Jim. "That wasn't a picnic for the last three days. Everyone busted their butts and stretched their minds."

"Mary said the same thing," said Fred.

"And it'll all be for nothing if the fifth S isn't practiced, and that's *sustaining* the effort. That's the hard part. The 5S process is the "ticket to play" Lean. If we can't hold the gains from 5S, we can't move forward."

"How do we do that?" asked Charles.

"We have a 5S audit team and a corrective action process. But in the end, the process will be sustained only if the operators enjoy working in their new environment, experience improved performance, and the job becomes physically less demanding. And so far, operator feedback's all positive."

Peter added his thoughts. "At the conclusion of the 5S events, I attend the team presentations. They always have some glowing comments about the experience, but the most telling line came from a team member when I asked about their impressions of 5S now versus prior to the event. They admitted they were skeptical, but after participating one team member said, 'Until you put the vest on, you can't appreciate the experience.' That comment convinced me to participate as soon as possible.

"Mike, go over the other Lean initiatives. I want to make sure everyone knows what you're doing."

"No problem. We've been using electronic kanbans and our inventory levels have been declining dramatically. Parts are automatically delivered as we consume the items. The planners like the system and want to move more items off MRP and onto Nocturne. The only downside, as Fred can attest to, is sometimes our purchase price variances and freight charges have increased due to smaller lot sizes and more frequent deliveries. But it's not a big issue. In the meantime our improved cash flow more than offsets the additional charges."

"It's great for manufacturing and accounting, but the new cost reports are creating havoc for sales and marketing," countered Steve. "The margin reports are a mess. The sales folce sees the new costs, which are much lower than last year, and they think we're ripping off their customers. They want to lower our prices. And now we have a lot of new products coming to market and we're having a hard time pricing them. The old formulas are useless."

"I agree," said Randy. "Our new product target costs were reworked by Mary's department and my guys are lost. They have a lot of make vs. buy decisions coming up and they're constantly asking for my help. I'm as confused as they are."

"C'mon guys," said Mike. "We've had a lot of classes for department heads and you never show up. In your absence, Mary tried to meet with your staff to explain the new reports, but only a few people showed up. Everyone's busy, but you have to let your people know how important it is to understand the new metrics. You've got to set the example. Peter's right. Once you spend three days on a 5S event, they'll know you're serious. Actions speak louder then words."

Steve shot back, "I wish I had time to attend classes, but I have a forecast to meet. Do you think I like being on the road all the time?"

"I'm not suggesting you do."

"When I finally spend time in the office, I'm inundated by meetings and product development issues. We also have a number of trade shows coming up and if I don't finalize the plans, we'll never be ready. I can't help it if you started this Lean program at the busiest time of the year. I'll do what I can to support you, but I can't take a week out of my schedule to attend class and a 5S event."

"I really need your support. We can get by without you participating in a 5S event, but you and your staff have to spend time in class to learn the concepts. You can't be the only area that doesn't know what's going on."

"That's hardly the case."

"Well, you have to help change it. Just like your guys joke about manufacturing, don't you think my guys make fun of marketing and sales? They think your area is a bunch of prima donnas that spend most of their time dining out with customers and living the good life."

"Take it easy, boss. It's not that bad."

"You don't understand. We have a great opportunity for all the departments to come together and solve some of the company's most pressing problems and, as a bonus, get to know each other better."

"Let's put this in perspective," said Peter. "Our first responsibility is to insure that the day-to-day business is taken care of. Any Lean disciple will agree that's the priority."

"I have no argument with that," said Mike.

"Good. Then to take this company to the next level, we have to devote a portion of our time to programs that'll provide us with a long-term competitive advantage. Steve, you need to delegate more of the day-to-day work to your staff. Examine your activities like the machine center did, and I'm certain you'll find a lot of waste. You must find time for Lean. It's our responsibility to profitably grow the company, and as a North American manufacturer, it won't happen using traditional methods. We have no choice."

"I understand the difficulty everyone's having with the new pricing formulas," said Mike, "but they have to understand, the economics of the company haven't changed."

"That's easy for you to say. They don't understand it," responded Steve.

"It's not difficult! Since overhead was removed from standard costs, product margins will be ten to twenty percentage points higher than before. If we used to make a fifty percent gross margin for a product, the new reports will indicate a sixty to seventy percent margin. The difference is the new report is now calculating a variable margin. It excludes a major cost component, overhead. Any price reduction will result in a direct hit to our bottom line."

"It's hard to break old habits."

"We can clear this up if we get everyone together for a Q and A session."

"I'll schedule a meeting next week," said Steve. "My guys have to understand the new reports or we'll have a mess."

"Randy, make sure your guys attend as well," instructed Peter.

"Sure thing."

"Mike, if our work standards simply reflect historical norms rather than what might be possible, what do my engineers do to correct everything?" asked Charles.

"Good question. The trouble is, no one knows what the process is capable of, whether we're talking about the machining operations or the assembly areas. Only with a cross-functional team methodically analyzing each area can we even begin to understand how much improvement can be achieved. Make sure your engineers participate on a team as soon as possible and I guarantee it'll be an amazing learning experience."

"I hope you're right."

"It never fails. They'll also realize that most of the improvements come from the floor personnel. Your engineers will have plenty to do to keep up with all the ideas."

"I'll make sure they attend the next class."

"Don't forget, even after the class you'll still have skeptics. The class won't accomplish much. They must participate on the floor teams, all of them. As someone from a world class company once told me, the only good engineer is one who gets weld dust on his forehead at least three times a day. You can't possibly know what's going on from behind a desk."

"I get your point."

"One more thing. I might as well drop the biggest bombshell of all. As Fred mentioned, we'll be freeing up a lot of space on the manufacturing floor. At some point I'll ask you to move the manufacturing engineers to the production floor."

"They'll quit before they do that."

"I doubt it. I'm not asking you to do it now. After they've been on a few teams, they'll realize they have to be closer to the action. You'll have to provide the initial push, but their resistance level will be much lower by then. It's an evolutionary process."

"I can't even imagine it. When will it happen?"

"Not for at least a year, so don't worry about it."

Charles breathed a sigh of relief.

Mike explained a number of other Lean initiatives in process and the other attendees reported on their areas.

Peter then wrapped up the meeting.

"Our progress with Lean over the last six months has been remarkable. Some of you have your doubts, and that's natural until you fully invest yourselves in the process and experience first-hand the improvements that can be achieved. We'll never achieve our goals without Lean. Your participation's critical."

The meeting was adjourned.

Randy and Steve chatted as they headed down the hall.

"So what do you make of all of this?" asked Randy.

"I don't know. Mike's gotten everyone into a frenzy and I haven't seen any measurable improvements yet. I don't believe those numbers. I'm surprised Fred's so gung ho."

"Me, too. He usually doesn't support anything unless there's a real financial pay back."

"What's gotten into him, it's so out of character?"

"When I get a chance I'll ask him about his new-found enthusiasm for Lean."
"Good idea. Let me know what he says."
"Will do; see you later."

Peter took Mike aside after the meeting.
"You're going to have to go out of your way to convince Steve and Randy of the merits of Lean. They both respect Fred and you should include him in your meetings. Once they understand how this will help our competitive position, they'll be your biggest support-ers. I just hope they come around as quickly as Fred did."
"Good idea. I'm sure Fred will be a big help. I'm worried Fred's going too fast in his area. I never thought I might have to slow him down."
"He'll be OK." They laughed and headed back to their offices.

26 Fred's Appeal

"Fred," said Randy as he noticed Fred looking for a table in the company cafeteria and waved him over.

As Fred approached, Randy pulled a chair from the table.

"I didn't even see you guys. Thanks. Fred set his tray on the table but hesitated to sit down.

"Well, have a seat," insisted Steve.

"Mike's joining me. He's still in line. Sure you still want me to sit down?"

Steve and Randy looked at each other. "Go ahead," said Steve. "We don't have a problem with Mike as long as he stays out of our area. Anyway, we wanted to know why you're so into this Lean stuff. What's changed?"

"Over here," said Fred as he waved Mike over.

"Hi, guys," said Mike as he took a seat next to Randy.

"We were just asking Fred why he's such a big fan of Lean now."

"I can't wait to hear that," said Mike.

"So tell us, Fred, what's the story?

"I've seen the initial results. The efficiencies of the work centers that've been 5S'd have gone up by five points. We haven't had a five point increase in years. And we hardly spent any money."

"Big deal, that doesn't mean anything to me," said Steve.

"It will once it's happening all over the plant. As

our set-ups improve, we'll change over more often."

"Why?"

"Because the lower set-up costs will justify lower lot sizes. And that means we can adjust quicker to changes in demand. The same thing will happen in assembly. It'll really help you out."

"That's great, since he can't forecast worth shit," said Randy, laughing out loud.

"Actually, it's not his fault he can't forecast demand," said Mike. "No one can. Unless we can respond quickly to changes, we'll never satisfy our customers."

"I'll believe it when I see it," said Steve.

"You gotta help make it happen," said Fred. "I'm beginning to understand Lean has more to do with servicing customers than achieving simple cost reductions. Imagine when our lead times are half the competition's."

"It'll never happen."

"Come on, Steve, don't be so negative."

"I don't want to get my hopes up. I thought you were excited about the cost reductions."

"I am. But Lean's a lot more than that. You're going to get lower cost product in half the time. That's what I'm excited about. It'll cost less because of speed, not because we've cheapened the product."

"Take it easy, Fred," said Mike. "We'll get a lot of benefits, but it'll take years. Let's not get ahead of ourselves."

"I know, I just want these guys to understand the end game and maybe they'll get a little more enthusiastic about it."

"I'll try to find some time for it, I promise," said Randy. "Now shut up and eat your lunch before it gets cold."

27 The EPS Hit

"What's the matter, Mary, you look puzzled?" said Tom.

"We've overlooked a major problem with the forecast," she responded as she dropped a stack of computer printouts onto the table.

"What?"

"During the last few months, Mike's kanbans have had a dramatic impact on inventory levels."

"I know. It's a good thing we provided for the obsolescence reserve last year. Is that what you're worried about?"

"I wish. There's more bad news, at least from a financial statement perspective," responded Mary as she took a seat at the table.

Tom grabbed his coffee mug, got up from his desk and joined her.

"Don't tell me we underestimated the obsolescence reserve."

"A little bit, but that's not the problem. If I'm correct, we've lost sight of the impact that improving inventory turns will have on the Income Statement."

"I'm not following you. What are you talking about?"

"You're not going to like it. Inventory turns for the first group of parts using kanbans have gone from 4.0 to about 4.4 turns in just the last few months. Mike said we wouldn't have to replenish our stocks for the first few months of the program and he was right."

"So what's the big deal?"

"Let me finish and you'll understand. The improvement in inventory turns doesn't seem significant, but it really is. I realized that when I was trying to forecast the quarter-ending Fixed Cost in Inventory account balance. Since we use a twelve-month moving average to calculate inventory turns, the activity in any one quarter doesn't have a significant impact. Also, since we're using electronic kanbans for only five percent of the inventory, it's difficult to move the overall turns average. As a result no adjusting entry will be required in that account for the first quarter, but that's misleading."

"Will you get to the point already."

"I'm trying to. Shut up for a second and listen. As we proceed through the year, expand the use of kanbans, and add more and more months of lower and lower inventory levels into the moving average equation, our inventory turns will accelerate. I forecasted full-year inventory turns and the resulting impact on the financial statements and realized the more successful we are, the greater the hit we'll have to earnings."

"I'm not following you, are you worried about larger inventory obsolescence charges?"

"No, no, it's an entirely different issue. Bear with me. In another month we'll be adding more suppliers to the kanban program, leading to further reductions in our inventory. Our twelve-month moving average inventory, the denominator to the inventory turns calculation, will continue to decline. In addition, the numerator in the inventory turns equation, cost of goods sold, is growing due to the sales increase. This phenomenon will continue, and in fact accelerate, throughout the year. I tested a few scenarios and we'll end the year with inventory turns of about 4.75 vs. our historical average of about 4.0 turns."

"And...."

"The improvement in inventory turns will reduce earnings per share by about three cents."

Tom took a big sip of coffee. "On top of the obsolescence charges we already reserved for last year?"

"Yep, the two items are independent."

"Go on. Use the whiteboard if it'll help."

"At the start of the year we moved $8,250,000 from our inventory at standard account to the new Balance Sheet account, Fixed Costs in Inventory. These were the 'extracted fixed costs' calculated by running the perpetual inventory twice, once based on full absorption costs and a second time based on variable costs."

"I know, I know."

"Boy, you're impatient today."

"What do you expect? The new forecast is due this afternoon and I've been waiting for you. We've got a deadline to meet. Go ahead and finish."

"I confirmed the opening Balance Sheet calculation by dividing last year's fixed costs of $33,000,000 by our inventory turns, which have historically been about 4.0. Fortunately, both calculations tied out. Then I forecasted our year-end Fixed Costs in Inventory Balance Sheet account by dividing our projected annual fixed costs, which are basically the same as last year, by the average inventory turns. We're just capitalizing fixed costs the same way we capitalize admin costs for tax purposes so it's an easy calculation. Based on a full year projection of 4.75 inventory turns, we'll only need $6,950,000 of fixed costs in inventory at the end of this year."

"That's quite a difference."

"And that's the problem. The difference between the beginning and ending value, $1,300,000, has to be charged to the Income Statement. After tax it's a three cent per share reduction in earnings from our current forecast."

"These Lean initiatives are killing us!"

"In one sense, it really has nothing to do with Lean."

"What do you mean?"

"The P & L hit is a result of improved inventory management. Any time inventory turns improve, the Income Statement is penalized. Lean just facilitates the improvement. With Lean Accounting it's much easier to project the impact over the next few years."

"Great, Lean makes it easier to see the bad news coming."

"Why are you such a cynic?"

"I'll tell you why. You and Fred are head-over-heels about this Lean stuff. Do you have any idea what I had to do to complete the year-end audit and support the cost system changes at the same time? I'm working my butt off and you two just keep throwing more shit at me. You're spending a lot of time collecting new data and working on the 5S stuff and now at the last minute you tell me about a forecast surprise. If you didn't spend so much time on all the new stuff, maybe you would've caught this sooner. I'm concerned you've forgotten what your priorities are, Mary."

"That's unfair. We all decided to make the changes. I've had a lot of extra work also."

"I warned you and Fred that we'll have problems, but you both ignored me. We're all doing too much."

"I didn't realize how overloaded you were."

"It's been difficult. I wish I could spend more time learning Lean, but someone's got to close the books around here. As it is, I hardly ever get to see my two kids anymore."

"I'm sorry. Hopefully, everything we're doing will eventually simplify things in accounting."

"Perhaps, but until they do, I need you to stay focused on your accounting responsibilities. I'm worried you're getting too caught up in manufacturing issues that are outside your area of responsibility."

"I'll tell Mike I have to tone it down. He'll understand."

"Thanks, now tell me, what's going to happen over the next few years if inventory keeps going down?"

"Sure. It's easy to calculate the annual impact to the P & L. We just divide the projected annual Fixed Costs by the projected inventory turns. The calculation provides the required year-end balance in the Fixed Costs in Inventory account. The year-to-year reduction flows through the P & L. Unfortunately, the biggest hits are taken in the first couple of years because the percentage improvement in turns is the greatest."

"So this goes on forever."

"Theoretically, as turns goes to spins, and then increases to infinity, the Balance Sheet account goes to zero." Mary demonstrated it with a graph on the whiteboard. "Eventually there'd be no inventory and all costs would be expensed. I ran the concept by Mike and he told me some world class companies actually expense all manufacturing costs since inventory levels are so low. In that situation it's a waste to flow everything in and out of inventory."

"Yeah, didn't he talk about that a few months ago."

"He reminded me that he did. I guess we just weren't grasping all of it."

"I guess I should've been aware of the potential impact as well. I'm sorry if I was a little short with you. The pressure's getting to me."

"Hey, don't worry about it. We were bound to miss something. We're moving pretty fast with the changes."

"That's never an excuse. It's our job to eliminate surprises. Go ahead and finish your explanation."

"Another way of looking at the problem is by imagining a company spending an entire year filling market demand by shipping product from inventory. Assume no production took place for the entire year and all inventory was consumed."

"That's not realistic."

"I know, but it's the best way to understand this. The company would have to record two year's worth of Fixed Manufacturing expenses on its Income Statement. The same expense would occur with a full absorption cost system as a year's worth of fixed costs would be included in the standard cost of sales and the current year's expense would be charged as unabsorbed overhead since no production took place. Either way, all the fixed costs built up on the Balance Sheet over the years have to be 'flushed' through the Income Statement as inventory is reduced."

"That makes it crystal clear. So how bad's it going to be?"

"The beginning fixed cost in inventory balance of $8,250,000 will shrink to about $4,000,000 over the next few years."

"I'm pissed we didn't anticipate this."

"Me, too. We all thought the obsolescence charge was the only impact of lowering inventory. We're not used to increases in inventory turns, so we never encountered such an entry. Also, we were so busy with all the other changes that we didn't think through all of the ramifications."

"I should have caught it."

"Don't be so hard on yourself. We all missed it."

"Thanks for the explanation. I'll go and tell Fred about it. How do you think he'll react?"

"Like you, disappointed he didn't foresee the charge. He'll also feel like he let Peter down."

"For sure."

"If anyone should've anticipated the charge, it was me. Let me know how it goes."

Tom headed to Fred's office. He wondered why calculation errors or oversights in accounting always resulted in a charge to the Income Statement and never,

ever did they result in what's called a "pick-up" or an increase to income. It was another one of the universal laws of business, and he hated it.

"Have you got a minute, Fred?"

"Sure, what's on your mind?"

"I'm afraid I have some bad news. We've overlooked the financial impact of an increase in inventory turns."

"I don't understand"

"We're gonna have a $1.3 million pretax hit by the end of the year."

"Son of a bitch! Who discovered it?"

"Mary."

"Is she sure?"

"Absolutely."

"How'd she find out?"

"She was working on the quarterly forecast update and had to develop new procedures for calculating the year-end Fixed Cost in Inventory. When she projected the full-year impact of increased inventory turns, she discovered it."

"I thought there wouldn't be much of an impact in the first year."

"Mike's kanban routines are working well and he's accelerating the implementation program. It won't take much of an improvement in inventory turns to create the $1,300,000 charge. Mary's confident it'll materialize."

"That's a three cent EPS hit. That'll wipe out sixty percent of our year-to-year earnings growth."

"I know."

"It's going to be hard to explain at this late date. I'd like to confirm the numbers with Mike before I bring Peter up to date."

"They won't change. Mary's already spoken to him."

"Damn, that's gonna hurt. How about next year?"

"Mary's working up the multi-year impact. This'll continue for some time. I'll get you the data by the end of the day."

"Thanks."

Tom left and Fred immediately called Mike.

"Can you come down to my office right away?"

"I'm in the middle of a meeting, Fred. Can it wait?"

"Hell no, I gotta talk to you right now."

Fred was pacing by his conference table when Mike entered.

"What's so important?"

"I just reviewed the full year forecast with Tom and we have to lower our EPS outlook by three cents a share."

"Why?"

"Because of the improvement in inventory turns. Damn it, Mike, why didn't you warn me about this?"

"I didn't think we'd move this fast with our suppliers. This usually doesn't happen until the second year. Is it a big problem?"

"What the hell do you think? Of course it is! Peter just gave the investment community and the Board an update last month. We'll look like jerks again. We need to put a positive spin on this."

"C'mon, we have a good explanation," exclaimed Mike, "and it's not spin, it's real."

"I know what you're getting at—cash flow."

"Absolutely. It's not a negative earnings surprise, it's a positive cash-flow surprise. Lean's about improving cash flow and asset utilization. Focus everyone's attention on the four million cash-flow improvement. The analysts will like that in their valuation models."

"Yeah. I'll let them know our new manufacturing strategies are ahead of schedule."

"That's the truth."

"I know, but it's a PR nightmare. I could see where the fear of reduced earnings can slow down a Lean implementation. Has that ever happened?"

"Of course, when top management's totally focused on quarter-to-quarter earnings. And it's a much bigger issue with public companies like Tricor."

"That's for sure."

"I was fortunate to cut my teeth on Lean with a private company where ownership managed for the long term. Our operating income was reduced by over twenty percent due to increased inventory turns. We could've slowed down the improvement in turns, but that's crazy."

"I can't imagine doing that."

"This'll be a real test for Peter and the Board."

"I'm not sure we want to be testing them. That's not our role. It would've helped if you had pointed this out earlier."

"I know. I didn't think we'd convert so many items to kanbans so soon. The P & L hit will get worse next year as we expand the program and have the benefit of lower inventories for all twelve months."

"Mary's calculating the long-term impact. Peter will want to fully disclose the issue."

"Let me know what she finds out. Is there anything else I can do?"

"Absolutely, what other surprises should I expect?"

"It won't happen for quite a while, and it's probably not material, but when Lean's fully functioning work in process inventories are dramatically reduced. Some companies just write off work-in-process and stop tracking it. I wouldn't worry about it now, but it could happen someday."

"Anything else?"

"Yeah, as we continue with 5S activities, we'll uncover equipment that's totally useless and should be sold or trashed. So expect some equipment write-downs. That's been the case at my other firms."

"Does it ever end?"

"Not really. The process strips away all unnecessary assets. It's a cleansing of sorts. Have you ever acquired a business?"

"Of course, but what's that got to do with this?"

"Bear with me for a moment. What was involved in the due diligence process?"

"We went through the inventory with a fine-tooth comb to make sure we weren't buying any garbage. We did the same thing for the fixed assets."

"Bingo. During Lean we're doing the same due diligence to our own company and uncovering all the garbage. Only we'll discover a lot more garbage than in an acquisition because we know our own company much better."

"I get the picture. I'm going to talk to Peter now."

"If I can help, let me know. I got you in this mess."

"It's ironic how we can disguise good news as a mess. I guess that's the irony of accounting."

"It sure is."

"If I'm not careful, I'll be a cynic like you. You're a bad influence."

"You're beginning to see how accounting can influence behavior in undesirable ways."

"I guess so. Now if you don't mind, I'm going to bring Peter up to date."

28 Peter's Response

While waiting for Peter to finish a telephone call, Fred thought about all the times he had to deliver bad news to his boss. He hated this part of the job and wanted to get it over with.

Peter hung up the phone and signaled Fred into his office.

"I just got off the phone with Joe. He's paranoid."

"What's his problem?" asked Fred as he slumped into the chair in front of Peter's desk.

"He's worried about the forecast. Joe's a terrific strategic thinker, but he's a real pain in the ass when it comes to the quarterly numbers. I assured him we were on target. Enough of my problems. What can I do for you?"

"I'm afraid Joe's right," said Fred as he glanced down at his empty notepad.

"What?"

"We just wrapped up the first quarter financial forecast and we have a problem."

"How bad?"

"We'll miss plan by three cents per share due to the improvement in inventory turns."

"I'm not sure I understand."

"Mike's programs are starting to take hold. By year-end, inventory will be down $4,000,000."

"That's great."

"Sort of."

"Don't drag this out, what's going on?"

"As inventory turns improve, we have to take a charge to the Income Statement, which in our case will be about $1,300,000 pre tax."

"You're saying our success is hurting us?"

"Precisely."

"I understood the inventory obsolescence charge, but this doesn't make any sense. Are you sure?"

"Absolutely."

"I don't have time to go through the details now. Let's go over it later so I can prepare for the pummeling I'll take from the Board. Is there any good news?"

"Actually there is. That's the irony of this. Cash flow will improve dramatically this year, and will continue to do so as we continue reducing inventory."

"I'll play that up with the Board. I'd feel more comfortable if you and Mike could come up with a plan to recover the three cents. Give it some thought and get back to me in a couple of days. I'll hold off talking to the Board until then."

"Will do."

"And, Fred, this better be the last surprise; otherwise we'll both be working somewhere else. Visit Mike's references and make sure you understand all the financial implications of Lean. If we can't predict what's going to happen, we'll have to slow down the implementation."

"I understand."

Fred returned to his office and thought about Peter's request. Sure, I could cut expenses by $1.3 million. It wouldn't be hard with nine months left in the year. Directing Randy and Steve to cut spending in the name of Lean is a surefire way to drive a wedge between them and Mike. I'm sick and tired of always having to cut expenses because of the quarterly numbers. Can't we ever manage for the long term? Just once, please. And why am I always the hatchet man? I need to brainstorm with Mike and come up with a better solution.

The following day Fred and Mike got together to discuss the problem.

Fred began, "Peter wants us to make up the profit shortfall."

"What do you think about it?"

"I don't like the idea of cutting expenses. It'll turn everyone against Lean."

"Your right. I can't believe Peter's first reaction was to ask us to make up the shortfall. I'm disappointed."

"It's your fault. You should've warned us about this. You're the Lean guru with a financial background."

"Yeah, I screwed up because we're generating four mil in cash flow. They say they're interested in the long run, but when push comes to shove, they're just interested in hitting the quarterly numbers. That's one of the reasons Lean gets derailed so easily, the short-term mentality of American business leaders. It's a show stopper every time. In case you can't tell, it really pisses me off."

"Settle down. You knew that would be the reaction. Cutting one point three million isn't that big a problem. If we don't do it, Peter has to go to the Board and explain the situation. Would you like to put the future of Lean in their hands?"

"Hell no. But wasn't Lean the Board's idea in the first place?"

"It was Joe's recommendation and he wants Peter out. Either he's setting Peter up or he really doesn't understand this. Do you think that makes a difference anyway?"

"I guess not. But if this is Peter and the Board's reaction, I'm scared of what'll come next. Once we start improving productivity, will they ask us to reduce headcount? It's amazing how quickly the no-layoff policy's forgotten. Believe me, it's easy for management to screw up an implementation, and I don't want to be part of that."

"Let's take care of the problem ourselves. Do you have any ideas?"

"Sure, but I'd hate to try it so early in the process."

"What is it?"

"At my last company, we improved lead times dramatically. Over a three-year period we reduced lead times from eight weeks to two weeks. Each time we ratcheted down the quoted lead times, we ate into the backlog, which created a temporary surge in shipments."

"Why was it temporary?"

"Even though we gave our distributors plenty of advance notice about the new lead times, they always took a couple of months to adjust their ordering patterns. I don't know if it was because they didn't trust us or because it took time to enter the new data in their ordering systems. In any event, the net result was a short-term gain in shipments as we reduced the backlog. Eventually, the distributors noticed the increase in their inventories and temporarily shut off orders to bring inventory in line."

"You think we can do that?"

"I think so. I'm converting one product line from batch to one-piece flow and it'll be implemented by the third quarter. The product doesn't account for a big percentage of sales, but it doesn't take much of an increase to offset the earnings shortfall. If we change lead times in the fourth quarter, we might get the earnings lift we need. Sales and marketing won't have any objections. They're constantly asking me to shorten our lead times."

"That's great..."

"Don't get so excited. It's temporary. Once the distributors believe our new lead times, we'll actually take a hit on shipments, but that probably won't happen until next year."

"So we're just postponing the inevitable?"

"Yeah, but probably for a few years since we'll constantly be adding products and further reducing lead times. So we should be OK for awhile."

"Then let's plan on it for now."

"That's your call. We'll make a final decision about the lead times by the end of the third quarter so we can notify our customers."

"I'll let Peter know what we're doing. I'll also develop a backup plan just in case."

"You better. I can't guarantee the timing. I told you before; there's some short-term pain with Lean."

"It's been nothing but a pain so far."

"Yeah, but you like it now."

"It makes sense."

"Let me clue you in on something else."

"I don't know how much more I can take."

"You'll like this."

"Go ahead," said Fred, leaning back in his chair and throwing his arms over the side.

"Lean frees up capacity and generates cash flow, but there's a time lag between the ever-increasing efficiencies and a company's ability to attract new business to use the capacity. There'll be a temptation to lay off personnel, but that would be a big mistake."

"You're saying we'll have another surprise?"

"No, costs won't be higher than usual, we'll just have excess labor. We'll be capable of much more output with the same resources."

"What do we do about it?"

"Look for acquisition candidates in about a year."

"Are you serious?"

"Very. We'll need more work. I'd look for a small, inefficient company that'd benefit from our Lean knowhow. It's never too early to start the search. If we play our cards right, we'll be able to pay for a good portion of the acquisition from inventory reductions."

"Sounds too good to be true."

"It's been done a lot by World Class companies. Lean becomes a core competency that can be leveraged."

"I can't wait until we're World Class."

"We have a long, long way to go. From an accounting point of view, we've spent most of our time on the cost system. There are a lot of other changes that have to take place in your area."

"Don't tell me we're going to have to get together again and discuss it."

"Of course. When can we do it?"

"How about next Thursday?"

"Fine with me," said Mike as he got up and headed out of Fred's office. "Good luck with Peter."

"Thanks."

29 Backlog Reduction

"What have you come up with?" asked Peter.

"I talked it over with Mike and he thinks we can offset the problem by reducing lead-times on our surge protector product line,"said Fred.

"Is that the one they're converting to a cell?"

"Exactly. By the fourth quarter, we'll be able to reduce lead times allowing us to accelerate shipments and eat into the backlog."

"Can we make up the entire shortfall that way?"

"We hope so. It won't take much of an increase in sales to offset the shortfall. And based on what I've seen, Mike will make the schedule."

"Sounds like you're beginning to like the young hotshot. Isn't that the term you used?"

"He really wants to improve results and I respect that. He also puts in extraordinary hours. I just wish he'd warn us about these surprises."

"I think he'll work out fine. Thanks for getting back to me so quickly."

"I need to ask you a question."

"Sounds serious, go ahead."

"If we didn't come up with a solution, would you really ask us to cut expenses to offset the impact of Lean?"

"Putting me to the test, aren't you? I don't want to jeopardize Lean either. I was hoping you'd come up with a creative solution. If not, we'd find the money in the corporate accounts. Cutting a million dollars wouldn't be too hard. I'd sacrifice one of my programs if I had to. Lean's too critical to our long-term survival."

"I figured as much."

"I have one question for you. If we're going to become world class, we have to implement Lean throughout the company, not just at this site. Do you have any ideas how we can do that?"

"I sure do. We need to put a Lean advocate at each of the other plants. Mary's already approached me about that. With Mike's support, and some training, she'd love to lead the Lean transition at our West Coast facility."

"She'd be a natural for it. Make sure she gets whatever training she needs."

30 Information Technology

A few months later, Mike was walking down the hall when Christy stopped him rather abruptly.

"Mike, we need to talk."

"What's the problem?"

"I can't keep up with the IT requests. I need your help."

"Do you have time to discuss it now?"

"Sure."

"Let's go to my office."

Mike was ecstatic that Fred fully supported Lean. One convert and only about a half dozen more key managers to go. It would take quite a while to convince sales, marketing, and engineering, but he thought Christy was fully on board. She was a critical player and Mike needed her support.

"Have a seat," said Mike as he motioned to Christy.

"Wow, this is amazing. You've taped off everything in your office. When did you do it?"

"I had to 5S my office and set an example. I might've gone a little overboard, but it gets the point across."

"I'll say, it's impressive. You have a spot for your garbage pail, stapler, tape dispenser …."

"Not nearly as impressive as when they sustain the 5S gains at a large machine center. So what's bothering you?"

"You know I'm all for Lean, it makes a lot of sense, but my staff can't keep up with your requests. It's impossible to plan my department's workload. I have a tremendous backlog of programming requests and your staff's throwing more and more work at us."

"Do you need some temporary help."

"That's not really the problem."

"So what is?"

"My staff's worried about rumors that they won't have a job after Lean's fully functional. They're concerned they're working themselves out of a job and I don't know what to tell them."

"We have enough IT work to last forever. It sounds like Mary's concerns a few months ago and you know how happy she is now. She's in the learning mode and interfacing with manufacturing more than ever. The same will happen with your area."

"I hate to burst your bubble, but my staff could care less if they're going to interface with manufacturing any more than usual. They want to keep up with the latest technology, including the Internet. If they don't, they'll become road kill. They know it and I know it."

"Don't they realize Lean will make us a more secure company?"

"They're not worried about job security at Tricor, they're worried about their IT careers. So when they hear rumors that MRP will be dismantled and we're going back to manual systems, they panic. You need to help me address their concerns, and soon."

"I understand, but their concerns aren't valid."

"That's easy for you to say. Perception's reality. You have to give me something to take back to them or we'll have a huge problem."

"You didn't let me finish."

"I'm sorry."

"First, let me address MRP. We all know we're trying to limit the use of the system. Day-to-day product flow eventually will be managed with visual controls on the production floor and electronic kanbans to our suppliers. We'll only use MRP for long range planning. Your staff'll have a lot of work in the transition."

"But what happens after that?"

"We'll streamline the supply chain."

"How?"

"By ramping up the use of electronic kanbans. We just started. We eventually have to link all of our plants as well. Your staff will get more exposure to the Internet and experience with an ASP model. And we're gonna expand the concept throughout the value stream to have a seamless flow of information from our customers, to Tricor, and to our suppliers. It's a tremendous challenge and a great learning experience for everyone. It's state-of-the-art use of IT resources."

"That's fine, but what else?"

"We'll need to build a management system for the electronic kanbans. At my last company, IT built a system that automatically updated kanban sizes based on fluctuations in demand. They also built systems to monitor blanket orders with pre-notification routines for expiration dates. The entire system automatically responded to changes in market conditions, and it wasn't done manually."

"That sounds pretty neat."

"There's plenty more. The entire work order system has to be revamped, bills of material have to be flattened to accommodate back flushing, the order receipt process has to be streamlined, and a host of new metrics will be developed."

"What role does my staff have in all of this?"

"We'll get a group of employees from all over the company, including IT, to tackle one item at a time. The teams will take part in kaizen events."

"What's that?"

"A concentrated three-to-five day rapid improvement event to improve performance. For admin processes, the team will use process-mapping tools to identify waste and then come up with ways to eliminate it. IT folks have the best training for process mapping and they usually come up with the most creative solutions."

"Give me an example."

"At one kaizen we reduced the customer order entry process from an elapsed time of twenty-three days to two days, in large part due to the efforts of IT."

"If Lean's about teamwork, then why haven't we been doing more of that? A lot of people feel left out and sometimes I do, too."

"Unfortunately, that happens. To get things going, we had to push some programming requests through the old fashioned way, via brute force."

"Why? It's pissed a lot of people off."

"We're not ready to begin kaizens. Training has to take place first and we're overloaded right now. I'm publishing a class schedule next week."

"It's about time. Why'd you wait so long?"

"There are two approaches. Educate everyone first, spend a lot of money, and have little to show for it, or educate a small group, implement, expand the education and further implement. I like the second approach. No matter which way you do it, someone gets pissed. You have to pick a path and go."

"What's wrong with educating everyone first?"

"It takes too long. By the time you implement, everyone's forgotten what they learned. It's too bad everyone can't participate from day one, but they get over it."

"I understand. But you gotta plan out your requirements or we'll never support Lean efficiently. I don't want muda in IT."

Mike smiled. "You're right. One more thing, Lean's routine in manufacturing but it's usually ignored in the admin areas. Software doesn't exist to support Lean in the office. What we're doing is leading edge. We'll be creating a competitive advantage and your staff's critical to our success. They've nothing to fear and a lot to learn."

"I hope you're right."

"Like everything else, it'll take time, but they'll come around."

Christy left Mike's office and he wondered which department head would be next in line to express their frustration. Would it be human resources because wage scales would be questioned when everybody in the plant is cross-trained and they want to know what's in it for them? Would it be engineering because it's time to relocate some people to the production floor? Or would it be the manufacturing supervisors because they feel like they're losing their authority as line workers are empowered to make decisions. Is it really worth all the aggravation? Mike thought about it for a couple of minutes. Of course, he decided, the gains are enormous.

31 Lean Accounting – What's Left?

"I'm looking forward to meeting with Mike today," said Fred as he took another bite of his bagel.

"That's quite a turn around," said Sheila. "Meeting with Mike used to cause you to lose your appetite, but you're doing a good job on that bagel."

Fred wiped some cream cheese off his mustache and continued, "We've had some good results with Lean. It's funny the way things have turned around. The more you understand Lean, the more you realize it'll help everyone."

"So Mike's not that bad after all."

"Don't rub it in. I met with Peter the other day and he wants me to start working with our investment bankers to develop an acquisition strategy. We're going to free up a lot of capacity and Peter wants to be ready for it."

"That's great. You love acquisitions."

"I sure do. I never thought Lean would lead to acquisitions. I thought it was about cost reductions. Boy, was I mistaken. I'll have more fun in the next couple of years than I've had in a long time."

"So what are you meeting with Mike about?"

"We're getting into some more accounting issues."

"Have fun," Sheila said with a big grin.

As soon as Fred got to his desk, he checked his e-mail and then called Mike.

"Mike, it's Fred. Do you want to get together now?"

"It's not even eight o'clock. I thought just us manufacturing folk came in early."

"I wanted to get going."

"Let me finish up with Jim and I'll be right over."

Mike walked into Fred's office and sat down at the table.

"What's the big hurry?"

"I don't mean to push you, but I want to know what else has to be done in accounting."

"Trust me, you have a long way to go."

"I can't imagine anything more controversial than changing the cost system."

"How about if I asked you to view accounting as you've always viewed manufacturing, as a production department?"

"I don't understand."

"Why's accounting any different than a manufacturing work center?"

"Uh?"

"You view work in the office differently than work in the plant. Accountants always want to measure manufacturing processes, but they never measure office activities, particularly their own. Did you ever stop to think that accounting's similar to traditional manufacturing?"

"How so?"

"You do a lot of batch processing just like traditional manufacturing."

"It's more efficient."

"Really? You have an end-of-month crunch and a bigger end-of-year crunch just like manufacturing. You repetitively perform rework and hardly ever get to the root cause. You have poor cross-training because of mandated control issues. Should I go on?"

"What do you mean by rework?"

"I'm talking about the journal entries you make at month-end. I bet the majority are correcting entries, which is really a repair function. How many times do you make the same adjustments at month-end without permanently fixing the problem? Do you track the number of journal entries each month, do you classify them as necessary vs. rework, do you have a continuous improvement process in place to eliminate all journal entries, do you graph the results and post them for everyone to see?"

"Aren't you getting carried away now?"

"Absolutely not. The true test of a world-class facility is whether a visitor can walk the plant floor and know what's going on by examining visual performance measures. The same's true in the office and I'm going to need someone to set the example. I'm counting on you to lead the way."

"Is it really necessary in the office areas?"

"Feeling threatened again? How come you have no problem putting standards in place for the operators in the plant, but when it comes to the office, it's off limits?"

"Our work's different."

"I doubt it. I'm going to post everything in the plant, and when I do, the first question I'll get is why aren't we doing the same thing in the office. And there's only one acceptable answer—WE ARE! We'll also be videotaping in the plant. That's the best way to improve work processes, but also the most threatening to the employees. Again, I tell them we'll be doing the same thing in the office."

"You're setting up cameras in accounting? Are you crazy?"

"Don't worry, we're not going to do any filming because that wouldn't work. But we'll develop process maps for admin activities which will serve the same function."

"So what's the big deal about that? We're always establishing standard processes."

"The method we'll be using is much more involved."

"How do you mean?"

"When we map a process, we'll get into the detail from how much time every step takes, to the number of keystrokes, to the walking distance, to the wait time, and to the total process time."

"Isn't that getting a little anal?"

"No, Lean's a war on waste. And it's been proven that about seventy-five percent of all our activities are muda. It's true for the office just like in the plant."

"Seventy-five percent! You're kidding."

"I'm not. We'll make dramatic improvements just like at my prior companies. We won't remove the muda all at once. It'll take years to eliminate the waste, but we need to get started and I need you to set the example."

"Give me some examples?"

"Sure. The cycle time to process an order was reduced ninety-one percent. The number of departments was reduced by seventy-six percent, the number of variances tracked were reduced by sixty percent, the number of minutes to process a purchase order was reduced by sixty-five percent, the number of month-end journal entries was reduced by fifty percent, the time for the month-end close was reduced by sixty percent. Do I need to go on?"

"Yeah. Go through the specifics."

"OK, I've got a good one. At one company, sales and marketing complained that the month-end financial reports were full of errors. Line item expenses were either charged to the incorrect account or the wrong department. Finally, the VP of Sales and Marketing demanded, as only he could, that the process be corrected. He refused to review month-end reports if they contained errors."

"So what happened?"

"The Controller's solution was to set up an additional inspection routine prior to issuing month-end results. I intervened and led a three-day mini-kaizen event where a team of ten employees flow-charted the process. Prior to the event, the accounting staff collected all sorts of data."

"Like what?"

"During the kaizen event, we created process maps for each path whereby an account number is assigned, such as expense accounts, inventory purchases, service requisitions, payroll, and one other I can't remember. We created five process maps. The data we prepared in advance allowed us to accurately record the activity at each step of the process, such as the number of expense reports per month or the number of invoices paid. Then the error rate for each activity was determined and the time and number of steps to make the correction were recorded. For all the activities we counted keystrokes, measured the distance walked to printers, and captured every nuance of the process."

"That's overkill. Counting keystrokes is ridiculous."

"Why is counting keystrokes any more ridiculous then knowing to the penny what a product costs, or measuring the speed of a machine, or precisely tracking purchase price variances, or performing a time study on an assembly operation? That's the kind of detail that's captured in the plant all the time. Don't we time-study everything out there? Why's it different because it's white-collar work? They're repetitive tasks that consume an enormous number of hours, yet we resist every attempt to measure them. And as we found out, they have high error rates."

"What'd you do next?"

"We noted the volumes, times, and error rates for each activity. Accounting tracked these for the prior month. That completed the first step, which we call the Current State. Then we developed the process map for the Future State. That's the fun part. The group brainstorms improvements. Included were two employees who had no involvement with any of the activities. These strangers to the process provided what's called 'fresh eyes' to the event."

"They didn't know anything about the process?"

"Nope. That's what's neat about it. They ask the most innocent questions which lead to the biggest improvements. After the brainstorming session, we developed an action plan to move from the Current to the Future State."

"Were there many changes?"

"And how. It's easy to compare the current and future states and identify the non-value-added steps, or the waste, in the original process. It was mind boggling how much time and effort was spent doing things simply because they had always been done that way, just like in manufacturing."

"So you gonna tell me how the account errors were eliminated?"

"To everyone's surprise, the team realized accounting hardly ever assigned account numbers. Purchasing entered account codes for inventory items, department heads, or their designates assigned account codes for services or supplies, etc. Because of the kaizen, marketing and sales realized they were creating all of their own problems by incorrectly assigning accounts when authorizing a purchase. They didn't pay attention to the account codes and assumed accounting would review and correct their mistakes."

"I could've told you that. It goes on all the time here."

"But we fixed it permanently. Sales and marketing's perception that accounting was screwing up was eliminated. Now they understood the process and took responsibility. They also asked for tools to error-proof the processes and insure correct account coding. Everyone's work content was reduced. We also moved people, printers, and workstations to improve the process, regardless of historical departmental boundaries."

"Did anyone get upset?"

"No, everyone was ecstatic. They didn't waste time fixing problems anymore. That's the difference with Lean. You achieve the best company-wide solution. Companies typically spend all their time attacking pieces of a problem, but never get to the root cause because they don't get everyone involved. Once we implemented the new processes, the participants supported it. They took ownership and made additional improvements whenever possible. And when the other departments found out they could organize a cross-functional team to help with their biggest headaches, they asked for kaizen events. This got the admin ball rolling."

"We use teams all the time. Everyone does. What's the big deal?"

"When you see a cross-functional team redesigning workflows in an intensive three-day effort, it's something special. The office kaizens are similar to those on the plant floor except there's no videotaping."

"I still don't see the difference."

"The difference is the rank-and-file are empowered to lead the events and implement the recommendations of the team. You're used to management-led efforts where everyone says what management wants to hear."

"That's not true."

"Oh, yes it is. It's human nature and everyone knows it. There's no buy in. The other differences are the measurements and continuous improvement efforts. After the new process was put in place, we monitored error rates and continuously made adjustments. We never accepted the status quo."

"It sounds like a lot of work."

"Of course it is. But when the employees start to initiate, and then lead the events, it becomes a self-sustaining process that's a huge competitive advantage. And that's the world-class difference. I'm counting on you to start it off in the office."

"Jeez, I can't wait. Is there anything else I can do for you?"

"Set an example by 5S'ing your area. Between you and me–it's a mess."

"I'm not putting masking tape all over my office like you did. It's stupid."

"You don't need to do that. I went a little overboard. But you'll need to remove everything you don't need, label every area, display all key metrics via visual display boards and sustain the effort. Also, if it makes sense, you'll need to move your staff where they'll be more productive."

"Enough already. We're fine as is."

"C'mon Fred, people can't sit in accounting just because they belong to the department. If it makes sense for the credit folks to sit with customer service, so be it. If accounts payable would be more efficient located in purchasing, let's do it. If parts invoicing should be with the picking, packing, and shipping area, relocate them. We did that at my last company and it made a huge difference."

"That'll be tough. You know how the engineers feel about relocating."

"It's a bitch. We all know that. And they'll resist as long as you let them. A healthy push is required to get them to move, but it has to be done."

"I think I've heard enough for one day."

"There's more. Eventually we won't track work in process inventory. We won't need to once we spin our inventory. With only one or two week's supply on hand, it doesn't deviate much. We'll carry a fixed dollar amount of WIP on the Balance Sheet, if any at all."

"That's one thing I'm looking forward to. It's tough to have a surprise with so little inventory on hand."

"Lean Accounting also means the elimination of transactions. Improvements happen on the manufacturing floor through physical changes, not in the Accounting department. You'll need to abandon the mindset that transactions improve results. World-class companies have measurements that are easily understood by the plant and are available immediately, rather than just at month-end."

"What will we use?"

"First Pass Yield, Overall Equipment Effectiveness, Takt Time, Absenteeism, PPM, Suggestions Per Employee, to name a few. The operators will track them visually at the work centers. We'll also track On Time Delivery per customer request, not per some arbitrarily imposed lead time, Percent of Workforce Cross-Trained, Percent of Workforce on Improvement Teams, etc. We want to select non-financial measures that lead to real improvements."

"I'm getting the picture. It can go on forever. Does anyone ever finish?"

"No. There are companies that've been at it for twenty-five years and still claim they find a tremendous amount of waste. It's a mindset that has to be maintained forever. It's one of the biggest competitive weapons a company has."

"And I assume one that can't be copied."

"Bingo. I just want to share one more story with you to demonstrate how difficult it is to see the obvious. I visited a manufacturing company that was on the road to world class. Just about everyone at the company, from HR to IT, from finance to purchasing, was flown to Denver to receive training in Demand Flow Technology. I met the President and Vice President of Operations and they shared their Lean successes with me. They had accomplished a great deal. At the end of the meeting, the President left to catch a plane and handed the VP of Operations a foot-high stack of checks to review and sign in his absence. I was dumbfounded."

"Why? That's pretty routine."

"It's muda!" said Mike slamming his fist on the corner of Fred's desk. "If the President personally reviews and signs each check, what does that say about the process? The necessary approvals should've been obtained prior to the commitment, not at the end of the process. It's analogous to final inspection in a plant, except it's worse, as the highest paid employee is spending time on nonvalue-added activity."

"Come on. In smaller companies the President or owner personally signs off on each check. It sets an example for everyone."

"Some example. He's telling his employees that the process leading up to his signature is a sham. If he wants to set an example, he should devise a process he's comfortable with, that prevents errors, and that precedes the commitment of funds. Anything else is a waste. Muda's all around us, and when given the opportunity we rationalize our behavior, even at the highest levels."

"I get your point."

"Are you ready to admit seventy-five percent of what you do is waste? Will you let a group of employees, many of whom know nothing about accounting, pick apart your processes? Are you willing to stand back and try not to defend everything? Will you be able to facilitate such a group and not offend another department head? That's what you have to do to get the ball rolling in the admin areas."

Fred took a deep breath. "I've got about two and a half years left, I might as well make them interesting. What choice do I have anyway with you around here?"

32 S&OP – Nine Months Later

The S & OP meetings were becoming more efficient each month. Forecasting was concentrated at the
product family level, eliminating a tremendous amount
of prep work. About half the parts were automatically
replenished via electronic kanbans and sections of the
MRP system were no longer used. Lead times were reduced in the fourth quarter as planned, and another reduction was expected within months. Finally, inventory
turns were accelerating and cash flow exceeded plan by
a wide margin. Even Wall Street bought into the strategy as the stock price hit an all-time high. But the storm
clouds were on the horizon. The coming year would be
tough.

Peter opened the meeting.

"We'll meet our financial targets this year, despite
the slight shortfall in sales, but it's only going to get
tougher next year. All indicators point to a slowdown
in our industry, and the key measure, the Book to Bill
Ratio, has turned south for the first time in three years.
We're going to have a hell of a challenge meeting expectations."

It was the same old speech. The upcoming budget
negotiations would be contentious.

After everyone presented their reports Peter turned
to Fred and asked, "How are we doing on the budget?"

"We're a few days behind schedule because we're

changing the format, but it shouldn't be a problem."

"What are you changing now?" asked Steve.

"You know, as part of our plan to move to a material-only cost system, we're removing labor from our standard costs this year. I sent out a notice last month."

"And ever since, my guys have been complaining. We've spent all year getting used to your new system and now you're changing it again. When does it stop? It takes too much time to get used to the new methods. We're not a bunch of accountants you know."

Randy jumped in to the conversation. "I agree with Steve. My engineers are frustrated. They're still confused and you're changing it again. And whenever I turn around, I've lost another engineer to participate on an improvement team. It's too much."

"C'mon, guys, my staff's gone out of their way to explain the changes. It would help if you let your guys know we'll make the numbers this year because of Lean. Why do you think they got a profit-sharing check last quarter?"

"Are you saying I didn't bust my ass?" responded Steve.

"Of course not. You work as hard as anyone, but when it comes to Lean you could care less. If you just showed some interest, your guys wouldn't fight the changes so much. This is the last major cost change. Work with me and let's get it behind us."

"Do I have a choice?" asked Steve.

"Honestly, no."

"My concern goes beyond the cost system," said Randy. "What's really pissing my guys off is the realization they'll have to move to the production floor soon. The market's getting tough, but there's always strong demand for good engineers. A number of them said they'll leave. Do they really have to move?"

"I'm afraid so, Randy," said Mike. "We've beaten this issue to death and need to get past it. It's part of the cultural change that's necessary."

"I'm warning you, we might lose some valuable talent."

"It's unfortunate, but we might. Don't expect a one hundred percent survival rate during the Lean transition. But, your attitude will determine how many people we do lose."

"I know exactly how you feel, Randy," said Fred.

"Do you?"

"My folks aren't exactly doing cartwheels over the changes? It's just as much a change for accounting and finance as it is for anyone else. Some of them hate to participate on the floor teams; they feel it's beneath them. Others despise the charts we've posted; they feel threatened."

"How did you get them to go along with it?"

"They had no choice. A couple of months ago, I went with Mike on a visit to a world-class company, and believe me, it was a sight to see. I'd hate to compete with them using traditional methods. You have to let your staff know this isn't about choice, it's about survival."

Steve continued with the objections. "I heard we'll take another Income Statement charge next year as the inventory continues to decrease."

"That's right," said Fred.

"That's great for cash flow, but if I have to cut my budget by a couple of million dollars, it's hard to get pumped up about Lean. Why can't we just reduce headcount in manufacturing now that we're so much more efficient?"

"We can't jeopardize our Lean journey by violating the no layoff policy," said Mike. "We've invested a lot in our personnel and we're building a long-term competitive advantage. It's our responsibility to utilize the workforce as we free up capacity. I told everyone at the outset that Lean would put tremendous pressure on us to fill the plant. That time is rapidly approaching."

Fred addressed the budget question. "We're all being asked to hold the line. Trust me, if not for Lean the situation would be a lot worse. Mary's group and purchasing have been working with Mike to identify insourcing opportunities to better utilize capacity. We'll save a significant amount next year, bringing more work in house."

"I'm glad everyone got their concerns out in the open," said Peter. "Lean's not a bottom up or middle out program, it has to be driven from the top through the entire organization. That's not just me, it's all of you. You need to lead by example. I'm disappointed more of you haven't participated in a 5S event. By the end of the next quarter, I expect every one of you to be part of an event. Your staff needs to know that Lean's here to stay. They're part of the program or they can find employment elsewhere. It's not negotiable. We all must walk the talk.

"I know you're all concerned about the coming year. When we embarked upon our Lean journey, I was well aware of the challenges we would face, especially as it relates to fully utilizing our production capacity. The softening in our markets has just necessitated an acceleration of our strategy. During the last nine months, Fred's been working with our investment bankers to identify suitable acquisition candidates and I expect to initiate discussions with a target company by the middle of the year. We'll use our manufacturing capabilities to the fullest. Fortunately, cash generated from improved inventory turns combined with the appreciated value of our stock will finance a reasonably sized acquisition.

"We must continue to support the Lean strategy. I'm counting on you to embrace Lean and drive it through your respective areas."

Some other topics were discussed and then everyone filed out of the conference room.

Randy and Steve met in the hallway.

"Peter's given us little choice in the matter," said Steve.

Randy responded. "No doubt about it. This isn't going away. I've done some reading on the Lean approach to product development and it's really different. You study nature and animals, it's really weird. I don't understand it. I don't know if it's for me."

"From what I've read, you can't argue with the results. Our competitive position will improve, which should make my job a lot easier. I'm already seeing some of the benefits from our shorter lead times. Maybe it's time we stopped fighting it."

"Fred sure did an about face in a hurry. He couldn't stand Mike last year and now he's Mike's biggest cheerleader. I respect Fred, so it can't be that bad. He's been trying to convince me all along, I just haven't had the time to devote to it."

"This'll be the make or break year for Lean. We're going to have to support it or leave."

"I know. I just hope Lean's everything they say it is."

Meanwhile Mike followed Fred to his office.

"Thanks for your support in the meeting," said Mike.

"I wouldn't have supported you if I didn't believe in Lean. Those guys are just where I was a year ago. They've been involved tangentially, and it's pretty scary and confusing until you dive in with both feet. I saw myself in both of them. They needed a good push and I think Peter provided that."

"You're right."

"Hey, it's impossible to understand it until you see for yourself. Accounting's beginning to operate on a different level because of some of the improvement efforts you led. They're excited about really affecting results, not just keeping score. They've told me their work is much more rewarding. And from a personal standpoint, I'm learning more about our operations than I ever thought possible. So thank you."

They shook hands and Mike left Fred's office.

When Fred arrived home that evening, Sheila was on the back deck tending the flowers. Fred went inside and filled two glasses with wine. He walked out to the deck, gently set the wine glasses on the patio table, and tip toed up behind Sheila and gave her a big hug. She turned around and they had a warm embrace.

"And why are you in such a good mood?"

"It was a good day. During our monthly meeting there was quite a discussion about Lean. Randy and Steve were against it and I argued for Lean. I was the Lean advocate."

"For the last few months you've been talking about Lean constantly. You've read every book you can get your hands on and have attended a couple of conferences. I should hope you believe in Lean, otherwise you've been wasting your time."

"I believe in it. That's the point. Watching and listening to Steve and Randy get so worked up was eerie, it was like watching me a year ago. Only I was worse."

"How did it feel watching them?"

"On one hand, I fully understood their frustration. It's normal to resist change. On the other hand, I was getting impatient, like Mike did with me."

"Don't tell me you acted like Mike."

"I hope not. Either you believe in Lean or you don't. And once you do, it's almost like religion. You become so immersed in it that it's easy to turn others off."

"Did you alienate them?"

"I hope not. I'll talk to them tomorrow and make

sure everything's fine."

"So, if you offended your two friends, why are you in such a good mood?"

"I didn't offend them. And that's not the issue."

"So what is?"

"A year ago I was thinking of retiring because of Mike and his Lean program. I couldn't imagine working with that bozo for three more years. Now I feel energized. I'm learning an entirely different way of doing my job. I'm having fun again, my staff's fully engaged, and Tricor's future is unlimited."

"That's great!"

"That's not all. I'll be working on acquisitions next year and I was even asked to speak at a financial conference about the challenges of implementing Lean Accounting."

"I'm so happy for you. Has this changed your retirement timetable?"

"Not really. I don't want to change any of our plans. And I still want to teach. But if I can do a little consulting on the side as well, I wouldn't mind."

"And what would you possibly be interested in consulting about?"

Fred ignored Sheila's question and handed her the glass of wine that had been sitting on the table.

Fred lifted his glass and proposed a toast.

"To Sheila, for her unwavering support during a trying year, thank you."

"Thank you, but to be honest, Lean just seems like common sense."